HAPPY HOCKWOOD

by Michael Roll

To Karen,

— I hope you get as much pleasure out of it, as I had writing it!

Michael Welling

ISBN: 978-1-291-42541-3

Copyright C 2013 Michael Wilton

No part of this publication may be reproduced, stored in a retrieval system, or transmitted, in any form, or by any means, electronic, mechanical, photocopying, recording, or otherwise, without the prior consent of the publisher.

This is a work of fiction. Names and characters are the product of the author's imagination and any resemblance to actual persons, living or dead, is entirely coincidental.

Contents

Introduction		Page	1
Chapter One	Something up at Oak Tree Cottage		2
Two	The lost hoard		11
Three	Careless Clara		23
Four	First move		39
Five	Down by the river		51
Six	Going to the races		63
Seven	Riding high		74
Eight	The brown rats move in		88
Nine	Out on a limb		99
Ten	Our postman		113

Introduction

When the animal wildlife in Hookwood is disturbed by the arrival of a young couple eager to set up their first home together in a derelict cottage, an inquisitive young rabbit called Startup decides to help out by finishing off their picnic lunch, donated by an old friend to celebrate the occasion. As a punishment, his mother Dora sends him out to look after his scatty friend, Clara Goose, while she moves house to escape the attention of the young couple's pet, a fearsome ginger cat.

After restoring the lifetime savings of his friends, dubiously acquired by Squirrel Nabbit, the rascally pawnbroker, Startup sets out to prevent Clara's nest egg falling into the hands of a smooth talking brown rat known as Captain Mayfair, who is looking for funds to back an uprising led by the fearsome King Freddie and his brown rat colony.

Regarded as a threat to the success of the Captain's plans, Startup is encouraged to fall under the spell of the brown rats secret weapon, a slinky looking rabbit called Lola, who is sent to ensnare the trusting rabbit and get him out of the way.

After a series of escapades where he is helped by his friends, Prudence and Wise Owl, as well as Puggles, the pig and Hedgie the hedgehog, Startup is involved in a running battle with the brown rats, and soon finds himself in direct confrontation with the arch villain, King Freddie himself.

In a gripping climax, Startup is caught up in a desperate hand-to-hand battle to the finish with King Freddie, in which his friend Wise Owl comes to his rescue, ready to sacrifice his own life in doing so.

Chapter One

Something up at Oak Tree Cottage

'I wonder what's up?' squeaked Startup, the irrepressible young rabbit, voicing the thoughts of all the animals drawing near to see what was going on. Something was up at Oak Tree Cottage, and soon the news was buzzing around the whole of Hookwood.

A large van was nosing its way up the lane towards the solitary cottage, and its uncertain progress was being broadcast from tree to tree along the route. It stopped at last at the foot of some old stone steps carved in the bank at the side of the lane, and several men and a boy got out, pointing to the sign and the cottage above.

There was some doubt at first whether they had come to the right place, for it was a funny tumble-down old cottage, set high above the sandy lane in the middle of the surrounding farmland, half a mile from Tanfield, the nearest village.

It had been empty for so long that many of the animals had come to regard it as their own. Indeed, the sparrows and starlings had been nesting under the broken roof tiles for many a long year, and Squire Nabbit, the rascally squirrel, had been storing his nuts in there as far back as he could remember. It was all rather unsettling, and some of the older ones amongst them were looking a little worried.

'I'll tell you what it means,' rasped Grumps, the one-eyed owl, making them all jump. 'Humans, that's who. Look!' He pointed with his claw, nearly losing his balance on the branch as he did so. One of the baby rabbits tittered, but the others shushed him and craned their heads expectantly.

Suddenly, there was a babble of talk from the lane. Car doors slammed, and a young couple ran up the steps, squeezing past the removal men in a hurry to get to their first new home together. The neglected state of the cottage did not seem to worry them. They chattered eagerly, happily taking in the state of the cottage and the overgrown garden, and the men in their aprons caught something of their mood and got to work, exchanging some friendly banter.

'They look O.K to me,' blurted out Startup, and some of the other rabbits privately agreed, but they didn't like to offend Grumps.

'Where are your manners, darling,' murmured his mother, Dora. His father snorted and gave him a cuff to show him who was boss. There was a sudden commotion at the top of the steps. The young removal boy was struggling with a wicker basket, and without warning a paw streaked out through the lid and clawed his face, making him drop the basket with a yelp.

'Oh, dear,' said Dora faintly. 'I think it's time I went home and got the supper. Come along, Startup, it is well past your bedtime.'

'But it's just starting to get exciting,' protested her son. 'Let me stay with Dad, just for a minute.'

'Ask your father then,' uttered Dora nervously, peering over the long grass.

After relaying the message, Startup turned back to his mother.

'Dad says, ask you. Please can I?'

He was talking to thin air, for Dora was already scuttling away down the bank, as fast as her trembling legs would carry her. Her husband, Ben, might not be afraid of cats, but she was, and she wasn't waiting a moment longer to find out what it was going to do.

It turned out to be a big striped marmalade cat that jumped out of the basket – the kind that stood no nonsense. He stalked stiffly up and down the path for a while, getting in everyone's way, nearly tripping up some of the removal men as they staggered up the steps with their loads.

Then one of the men fetched out the new owner who sat the cat in a makeshift box and told him not to move, in a very severe voice. The cat merely blinked disdainfully, shook his ruffled fur, and began to lick his front every now and then, while casting a sleepy but watchful eye over the scene.

The sight of the cat waiting at the door seemed to unnerve the young lad, and every time he arrived with a load, he set it down hurriedly and shot off again, afraid of being clawed. Soon an odd collection of furniture and boxes began to pile up. There was so much in the end that when the young owner appeared from upstairs, he found he could hardly get out, and the next removal man who followed up found his way blocked. It was a fine old mix-up.

Startup nudged his father and pointed gleefully, but Ben shushed him and got out his pipe. It was just beginning to get interesting, and he didn't intend to miss a thing.

Soon, two more removal men who were backing up the path with a settee bumped into the obstacle and came to a sudden halt. After a lot of dithering, word was passed down the line to stop bringing up any more loads. But by then men were going bumpity bump, like a crowd of goods trains backing into a siding.

Something had to be done. The removal man in charge scratched his head, and looked around for orders. But it was the cat who unknowingly supplied the answer. Getting bored with the whole proceedings, he leaped over their heads onto the porch and strolled up the short section of nearby roof and disappeared through the open window.

At last managing to squeeze out through the doorway, the young owner caught sight of the cat and it gave him an idea. He waved at the removal men and pointed up at the window. At first they nodded, grinning and smiling politely in turn. Then when the meaning dawned, their smiles faded and they looked around for a volunteer. As if by common consent, their eyes strayed towards the young lad who immediately stopped laughing, and turned to run for it. Before he could get far, he found himself hoisted up on the porch with ease by a big burly fellow, and there he crouched, his foot wedged between two split planks that made up the porch roof, begging to be let down.

Instead of giving him a hand, one of the men lifted up a chair and told him with a guffaw to sit on it, while he had a chance, because there was a lot more coming his way.

The men were a good natured lot, anxious to get finished, and one of them even climbed up next to him, with one leg braced on the porch to help ease the load, and heave the heavy items through. First came a table, then a kitchen cabinet – which the lad told them earnestly would never go through in a month of Sundays, but did - and so it went on – it was unbelievable what was going through that window.

'What are those funny lumps of wood for?' asked Startup, greatly puzzled, thinking of their own cramped burrow.

'For goodness sake,' spluttered his father over his pipe, not wanting to show his ignorance. 'Stop your chatter, I can't hear what they're saying.'

'Golly, do you understand human talk?' Startup was most impressed.

His father merely coughed importantly.

After that, Startup tried to listen with more respect, although it still made no sense, so he just watched in case he missed anything.

He needn't have worried. Nothing seemed to be happening. Everything had come to a halt, and the men stood around shuffling their feet, waiting to get off to their next job, while trying to avoid the reproachful looks of the young woman who had come down to find out what was up.

'It's not our fault,' the man in charge seemed to be saying, waving his arms apologetically at the pile on the doorstep. 'We've done the delivery as we promised, and that's what we've been paid for, begging your pardon, ma'am.' He touched his hat awkwardly, backing down the path. 'That cat of yours has gone and made us late for our other move over Packham Hill way. We only did it as a special, to fit in the two jobs, like.'

Behind him, the men were already taking the hint, and were scurrying down the steps like schoolboys let off early.

'Oh please, do stay!' the young woman was imploring, but she was talking to thin air, and soon there was only the sound of a spluttery exhaust to remind them that there had been anyone there at all.

The woman turned away and took a look at the furniture jammed in the doorway. It was suddenly too much to bear, and with a wail she threw herself into her husband's arms.

'What's she saying?' whispered Startup.

'She's a bit upset,' replied his father somewhat unnecessarily.

'What's she saying now?' asked his son after a fresh cry of anguish was heard.

'I think she's telling him she can't find a kettle...' answered Ben after a long pause. Then he added thoughtfully. 'I wonder what she wants that for?'

Startup was nonplussed. That was the very question he was going to ask himself.

'Isn't there anything we can do?' he wrinkled his nose.

'Do?' repeated his father crossly. 'We don't *do* anything. You don't help humans – you just keep out of their way,' he explained gruffly. 'Humans aren't like us,' he drummed his back feet in emphasis. 'They're different,' and he nodded, as if that answered everything.

'Oh,' said Startup, not entirely convinced. 'Perhaps she might like some parsnip soup. That's nourishing.' It was a word he'd heard his mother use, and it sounded important.

'No,' snapped Ben, getting nettled. 'That's my supper you're talking about - and if you're going to carry on making that sort of remark, we'll end up as rabbit pie. Now, be quiet, I can't hear what's happening.'

He puffed furiously to concentrate, but the voices were much quieter now, and it was difficult to hear anything. The young man was trying to calm down his wife, at the same time casting quick glances around to see what could be done. Everything was in such a fine old mess, it was obvious he didn't know where to start. Fortunately, he was saved from making a decision in an unexpected way. Suddenly, there was a loud 'hallo' from the lane below, and a big jolly woman clambered into view, clasping a large hamper.

Her arrival made an instant impact. It was as if a fairy had waved a magic wand. At the sight of the hamper, a smile of heartfelt relief lit up the young woman's face, and she rushed forward to greet her friend, clasping her with open arms, and doing a little dance at the top of the steps.

It was all too much for Grumps, the one-eyed owl, who had stayed on as a stern act of duty. Outraged, he flew away muttering darkly, 'No good will come of this.' But Startup watched entranced. He was so taken with the fun and gaiety, he nearly joined in himself, but his father managed to grab him just in time.

Instead, they crept along, following after the visitor as she enthused over the 'gorgeous' garden. In fact, the friend, called Olga, became so ecstatic over the jungle matted lawn and the half hidden flower beds, that Joan, the young wife, almost began to believe it herself. Her husband, George, was only too willing to believe anything at this stage, and thankfully humped the hamper along after them.

He was in the act of dusting down some deckchairs, and started carrying them across the grassy wilderness when he almost trod on the two rabbits. But they were so agog at the sight of all the delicious food being spread out, they didn't see him until he was almost on top of them.

Ben looked up wrathfully, and Startup gave an impudent flick of his back legs before hopping after his father, who led the way trying to appear dignified.

George was so taken aback at the encounter, he nearly dropped the chairs. Where he came from there wasn't a rabbit to be seen for miles, and now to stumble upon some suddenly like this made his day. He stood there, savouring the moment, feeling that at last this was where they belonged. It was all bound up in that marvellous feeling of owning his own house for the first time. He was so wrapped up in his thoughts that the others had to call him several times, before he realised they were there.

As he was arranging the deckchairs, he told his wife rather sheepishly that he had just seen some rabbits.

'Rabbits?' laughed the jolly lady. 'Remind me to let you have a recipe for rabbit pie, my dear. It's delicious.'

At her words, the very bushes around them seemed to rustle with the shock, and not far away old Ben stopped dead in his tracks, causing Startup to bump into him.

'D'you hear that?' squeaked his father in a fury. 'Rabbit pie, indeed. That's what comes of being too friendly, you mark my words.'

His outburst made Startup do a backward somersault in astonishment. He hadn't seen his father get so worked up since the day he sat on a pitch fork.

Old Ben puffed so hard on his pipe, he almost disappeared in a cloud of smoke. Then he poked his head out and jabbed at Startup with the stem. 'You keep away from Oak Tree Cottage, d'you hear? Or you'll end up in a pie as well. Delicious indeed,' he snorted. 'That's all we need - I'm going home for my supper.'

'But what about all that food, dad?' squawked Startup.

'I'll go back in the morning when they're still in bed and bring some back – that's if there's any left over,' grunted his father, kicking moodily at a passing grasshopper.

The offended insect hopped away clicking indignantly, 'What a rude rabbit!'

Young Startup couldn't help thinking longingly of all that food lying around, like unclaimed luggage at a lost property office. The more he thought about it, the slower his progress became. Every now and then, he would stop and have a thoughtful chew, and he soon dropped well behind. Then as if rehearsing his defence for later on, he struck off rather virtuously on what he decided was a short cut home. By a strange coincidence he found himself back in the garden again, close by the grown-up picnic party.

Hallo, he thought to himself, how did that happen? Then in a polite aside, so as not to disturb anyone, he mused, 'While I'm here I suppose I'd better make sure nobody's moved the hamper, in case they've lost it. After all,' he added to himself brightly, 'everyone knows that rabbits are good at looking for lost hampers – 'specially...' he nose twitched, '...when they've got lots of tasty things like lettuces and carrots and cabbages and things...' His back legs did a little dance in anticipation, as he edged forward.

He needn't have worried. In fact, there was so much food left that the young couple and their visitor lay stretched out contentedly, leaving half the contents of the hamper still untouched. Young Startup was just in time to see the jolly lady get up a little reluctantly and say good-bye. When he crept up for a closer look, his eyes grew as round as saucers at the sheer volume of food scattered around.

As he watched completely mesmerised, the young woman returned and gazed up at the cottage as if seeing it for the first time. Even as she looked, a tile fell off the roof with a clatter, and an upstairs window flew open, displaying half broken panes of glass and peeling paint.

'Oh, George, what have we taken on?' she wavered with sudden doubt.

But George smiled blissfully with complete assurance. 'Don't worry, my love, we've plenty of time. Just think what it will look like in ten years from now. And what with all that lovely food we've been given thrown in – why, we won't have to buy anything now for weeks and weeks.' He stretched back and shut his eyes with relish at the prospect.

It was too good an opportunity to miss. Startup took a deep breath and made a flying leap into the hamper. Although he couldn't understand a word the grown-ups were saying, he agreed with the sentiments all the way.

The young woman had her own ideas on the subject. 'Dear George,' she said sweetly. 'If we have to wait that long, we'll never get any of our furniture inside.' And with a determined toss of her head she made for the front door.

'Hey, wait for me.' George got up hastily, and as he uncoiled himself, he accidentally slammed the hamper shut as he followed her in.

Clunk. After the initial shock of finding himself trapped inside, Startup felt he had to make the best of it, and began to fortify himself with a few snacks to help him through whatever hazards that lay ahead.

It was an extremely full and outsize bunny that met George's shocked gaze when he came back to collect the hamper later that evening.

'Here!' he blinked in disbelief at the empty packets scattered around. 'The little blighter's scoffed the lot!'

George was not amused. No longer did he regard rabbits in the same rosy light that he did only a few hours previously. After a long tiring evening clearing up, he was looking forward to a nice sit down, and a welcome snack to go with it.

Luckily for Startup, he was in no condition for chasing rabbits. By the time he had collected his wits and made a grab at the cheeky fat culprit, the rabbit just managed to ease his portly frame over the top of the basket, and stagger away into the welcoming darkness.

In the event, his greediness was his undoing. When the exhausted rabbit finally arrived home he immediately got stuck in the entrance to the burrow, and had to wait until morning when his scandalised father was able to dig a tunnel out to free him.

Chapter Two

The lost hoard

Startup was feeling rather uncertain next morning. Uncertain about his father's temper, uncertain about what his mother would say when she saw the big hole in the front door, and above all uncertain about his tight, fat little tummy that was feeling very, very uncomfortable.

He trailed around listlessly until the flip flop of his paws on the sandy floor sounded so loud that he crept into a corner and curled up. Unfortunately for the naughty bunny, the aroma left behind from all the food he had eaten seemed to cling to him, and the smell wafted through the burrow and drew his father and mother like a magnet.

Ben confronted him, secretly furious that Startup had eaten all the delicious food he had been hankering after himself. What was more, he could sniff the evidence, for it was unmistakable. He could even pick out the different flavours like juicy lettuces and carrot tops and yes, the last one that left him all frustrated could only be strawberry flan.

Just as his father was working himself up into a state, his mother put him off his stroke by joining in. Feeling guilty about leaving Startup the night before, Dora took Ben aback by accusing him of leading his son astray.

'If you'd have found me a new home as I asked you, with a bigger entrance – like my friend Priscilla has on the west bank – none of this would have happened.'

Ben muttered darkly to himself. His views on his wife's friend, Priscilla, would have filled a book, but he didn't have a chance to air them.

His wife held up a paw to stop him interrupting. 'All you're interested in is meeting up with your friends down at the Dandelion Inn - I know what you get up to...'

Startup found he couldn't stand the sound of their voices any longer. It sounded like thunder and was making his head ache, so he crept out of the burrow, keeping his head down and hoping that nobody would notice.

He needn't have bothered. His mother was in full flow, just beginning to enjoy herself, and bringing out all the little complaints that had been vexing her over the years, till her eyes shone with righteous indignation.

'...and another thing...' she accused the by now bewildered Ben, who was beginning to hanker after his rabbit tobacco to sooth his shattered nerves, '...you're not catching me living here any longer, now they've got a cat prowling around outside. Why, it's not safe to go out at night anymore...'

Outside, the morning air smelt fresh and wholesome, and already Startup was beginning to feel a shade better. He poked his head up cautiously and his nose twitched appreciatively. It was going to be a beautiful day after all, he decided.

Even the smell of fried eggs and bacon wafting across from the cottage failed to upset his tummy much to his surprise, and he began to perk up. He hopped forward, telling his tummy that although he knew there wasn't any room for any more food inside, there couldn't be any harm in having a look.

He was so engrossed in his thoughts that he bumped into Squire Nabbit, the rascally old squirrel, who had made a fortune out of swindling the animals out of their savings, by posing as a self-styled honest pawnbroker.

'Oh, it's you, young Startup, is it?' said the squirrel, peering short-sightedly through his spectacles, his eyes worn out with counting piles of nuts.

'Hello,' said Startup cheekily. 'Are you after some breakfast as well?'

The Squire brushed his whiskers importantly. 'Good gracious no. I have other more important things to think about. Go away, young rabbit, and don't bother me.'

Then he turned thoughtfully. 'No, wait...there may be...ah, some trifling service you can oblige me with...' Then he rephrased his remarks rather pompously. '...or should I say, with which you can oblige?' He paused and preened his whiskers, regarding himself as something between an elder statesman and an international banker.

Startup just snorted and gave a sideways kick of derision.

Seeing that the rabbit was not paying attention, the Squire added cunningly, 'That is – if you think you are strong enough.'

The challenge was too much to resist. 'Me, strong enough? Strong enough for what?'

'Oh,' said Squire nonchalantly, 'just a little something I have to collect.' He waved a careless hand. 'Nothing very strenuous, of course. After last night, I don't suppose you're feeling much up to it...'

Startup looked at him suspiciously. The other animals might call Squirrel 'old nutball', but there wasn't much he missed.

'You've heard about the humans then.'

The Squire jumped nervously at the mention of the word. 'I believe that's what you call them.'

'Are you trying to tell me that it is something to do with the cottage?' asked rabbit, with dawning understanding.

'Just so.'

'Don't tell me you've lost something again,' pressed his inquisitor.

The Squire coughed. 'How did you know...I mean, I haven't so much as lost them, as mislaid... an investment, you might say.'

'Oh, your nuts,' decided Startup.

'I am no such thing,' spluttered the other indignantly.

Startup twitched impatiently. 'I meant, is it your nuts you've lost?'

'Mislaid would be a more appropriate term,' corrected the Squire pompously. 'I know *where* they are...it's just that I can't seem to get at them as easily as I used to.'

'Nor can any of the other animals you pinched them from,' said Startup, without thinking.

'Pinched them?' repeated the Squire in outraged tones. 'How dare you! I've loaned good money against those nuts. They represent my entire savings.'

'You can say that again,' chirped Startup. 'That's what all the other animals thought as well.'

'It's not my fault they couldn't repay their loans,' said Squire virtuously. 'That's what good business is all about.' He hesitated. 'Or should I say...'

Startup regarded him coldly. 'Well, if you can't get them, how do you think I can?'

'My boy,' said the Squirrel, placing his arm around him cordially. 'I see we're talking the same kind of language already.'

Five minutes later, after squirming through the long grass, the squirrel crawled cautiously up to the front porch of the cottage and inched his way forward carefully, only to find to his mortification that Startup was standing up in full view behind him.

'Get down, you young idiot,' he breathed fiercely, tugging at the rabbit.

'I say, what are you doing down there, Squire?' asked Startup brightly. 'It's all right - they're both upstairs, I can hear them.'

'Just so,' whispered the squirrel nervously. 'All the same, you can't be too careful, I always say. Come down here, so I don't have to shout.'

'Aren't they up in the porch then?' Startup carried on in his breezy way, peering up into the recess. 'That's where you usually keep them.'

'Who told you that?' yelped the other. 'I've never told anyone, ever. Nobody could possibly know.'

'Oh, that,' laughed Startup contemptuously. 'We often used to watch you creeping down here with your nuts. It used to be our standard exercise in tracking.' He nearly added that all the very beginners were started on it, but decided that the Squire's face was turning puce enough, as it was.

'Oh,' was all the discomforted Squire could manage.

'Yes, well aren't you going to get them?' Startup offered a hand. 'There's a ledge at the top, I expect they're still there. Go on, I'll keep watch.'

'I er...ouch!' Squire Nabbit clutched his leg dramatically, and gave what he hoped was a convincing groan. 'I do believe my old war wound is playing up again.'

'I thought you were too old for that last battle against the stoats?' Startup gave it a friendly prod.

Squire glared at him. 'You young bounder...!' Just in time, he remembered his awkward predicament and laughed weakly. 'You...playful little...bounder - always...bounding all over the place. What about jumping up there for me, and passing down a few nuts for poor old Squirrel, eh?'

Startup climbed up obligingly. 'Would if I could,' he called down at last, 'but someone's nailed it all up. Sorry, but you've had it.'

'What!' screamed Squire, unable to believe his ears. 'They can't have. You must be looking in the wrong place. What would they want with my nuts?'

'Perhaps,' said Startup helpfully, trying to remember another difficult word he'd heard his mother use once, 'they're vegenarians – you know, nut eaters.'

'Stuff and nonsense.' The Squire failed to see any humour in the remark. 'They're just as likely to have us for lunch if they had the chance – which reminds me,' he glanced around fearfully. 'I don't think this is the best place to discuss the matter any further.' And with that, he darted back into the long grass, leaving Rabbit on his own.

Startup stayed on the porch for a while, partly to show he wasn't afraid, and also because he became distracted by the dancing pattern of shadows on the front door, caused by the rising sun. He became so interested, he tried to capture the darting shadow with his paw without success, and was still sitting there enjoying his game when a face appeared at an upstairs window and looked down in amazement.

'Would you believe it – it's that little devil again!' said George wrathfully, forgetting he was holding up the settee, and dropped it on his toe. 'Ouch.'

'You've dropped it again, George,' said his wife sighing. 'Did you mean to block up the whole of the landing?'

'No,' said George shortly. He was getting tired of moving the furniture around, and seeing that rabbit again revived all his feelings of annoyance at finding the picnic hamper empty. 'I'll get it this time,' he muttered, reaching for his battered looking shotgun. It was given to him as a joke by a friend who couldn't get rid of it, and although he hadn't managed to fire it in anger yet, he felt rather like a big game hunter just by holding it in his hands.

His wife paled at the sight of it. 'You're not seriously going to use that, are you darling?'

Her questioning about his ability made him all the more determined.

'Why not? I'll show the little blighter.' And with that, he brought the wavering barrel up to the window sill.

His wife rushed forward. 'Wait, you can't fire that here.'

'Who says I can't?' blustered George.

'Because,' she giggled, 'you haven't opened the window.' Then she caught sight of the rabbit, still amusing himself by holding up his paw up to cast a shadow on the door. 'Oh, George, you weren't going to harm that poor little rabbit...?'

George squirmed under the accusation. 'That poor little rabbit, as you call it, scoffed all our picnic lunch last night.'

'But look at him, darling. He's so sweet. He's doing a little dance.'

'He'll be doing more than dance when I get hold of him,' promised her husband.

'George, I absolutely forbid you to hurt him. Why, he's just a baby.'

With a sigh, George reluctantly put down the gun. 'I suppose you're right,' he admitted. 'What's he up to now?'

Startup was getting bored with playing shadows, and he got up to have a closer look at the boarded off porch roof.

'He's trying to get into that hole I covered up,' reported George puzzled. 'What on earth is he doing that for?'

'Perhaps he's left something there. Don't forget those animals have had the place to themselves for so long,' murmured his wife, pressing her nose against the window to get a better view. 'Oh, George, do go and see. I'll be putting the kettle on.'

'All right,' agreed her husband, secretly relieved at the prospect of getting away from the drudge of unpacking. 'If you insist.'

When he arrived downstairs, Startup was busily tugging at the corner of a loose board and gave a squeak of satisfaction as it crumbled and fell off.

The next moment, there was a furious chattering noise and the agitated figure of Squire Nabbit dashed out of cover to get at his nuts. With a greedy shove, he thrust the young rabbit aside and plunged at the opening.

Left to get on with clearing away upstairs, George's wife came across the gun and screwed up her face. 'Nasty dangerous things,' she said, and propped it up in the corner of the bay window, out of sight. As if agreeing with her, the gun slipped sideways and went off, blasting a hole in the floor.

The force of the explosion sent pellets straight down through the porch roof, and a cascade of nuts immediately poured down on the Squire, pushing him effortlessly out of the way, like a cork from a bottle.

'Aaah!' he howled, disappearing out of sight under a growing heap of nuts, that were growing bigger and bigger by the minute. The force of the impact tossed Startup high in the air, and he found himself landing on something unexpectedly soft.

Startup couldn't help rolling back in a fit of giggles. 'Did you find the nuts then, Squire?'

There was a curious rumbling sound beneath him, followed by a roar of laughter like Niagara Falls, that caused him do a somersault in surprise. After recovering, he realized with a sudden shock that was sitting on the shoulders of the man mountain himself.

George looked down at him, and grinned in spite of himself. The sprawling rabbit presented a comic mixture of grace and impudence. Catching sight of the squirrel's head emerging from the sea of nuts, he heaved himself up and freed the squirming animal, setting him down gently on the ground. Without stopping to see if his waistcoat was straight, the squirrel made a bolt for the nearest tree and vanished in the depths of the foliage.

Even Startup thought it was time to move on, and hopped around the corner leaving George to scratch his head at the problem it left him.

Seeing that George was occupied, Startup hurried away to find the squirrel. 'It's all right, Squire,' he called up reassuringly. 'It's only me – Startup.'

A furry head poked furtively through the leaves. 'Are you sure?' it quavered. 'I feel so poorly, I do so.'

'There's nothing to worry about,' soothed Startup with a private grin. 'As long as we move fast, we can do something about it.'

The furry head came out a little further. 'Do something about what?' it cried. 'Oh, my nuts, my beautiful nuts!'

'Leave it to me,' encouraged Startup. 'If we hurry, we can get them all back.'

The squirrel nearly fainted at the news. 'How? I mean, I'll do anything....'

Spurring him on, rabbit said soothingly, 'Don't panic, we've got about five minutes before he comes back with a wheelbarrow.'

'Five minutes?' uttered the squirrel faintly. 'Is that all?'

'Now, there's nothing to it,' said Startup airily. 'You just hold the sack and I'll kick the nuts into it with my back legs. Of course...,' he pondered, glancing sideways to see if the squirrel would believe him. But the furry animal was drinking it in pathetically. '...of course,' he repeated casually, 'it might be a bit difficult kicking the nuts in - and dealing with the cat at the same time.'

'Cat?' shrieked the Squire. 'You didn't say anything about a cat.'

'Didn't I?' said Startup innocently. 'Oh yes, there's a big ginger cat – a rather fierce one, they tell me. I'm told he doesn't like squirrels over much – but that wouldn't worry you, would it?'

The head disappeared with a wail.

'The only solution...' said young Startup slowly, as he saw the squirrel's head creeping back with a faint glimmer of hope, '...no, that wouldn't be any good...'

'What wouldn't, what wouldn't?' gasped the Squire frantically. 'I'll do anything...'

'No, that would be too expensive...'

'How much?' clamoured the Squirrel, like a drowning swimmer going down for the second time.

Startup looked up at the sky reflectively. 'Well, if you work out how many nuts anyone could carry...and if I rounded up a few friends...we might be able to get some of them back...but it would need an awful lot of friends...and they would need an awful lot of persuading...'

He cocked his head on one side. 'Did I hear a wheelbarrow?'

'Name your price, but do something,' implored the quivering animal. At that moment, he looked quite unlike any elder statesman or international banker you might imagine.

The young rabbit sighed artistically. 'I have a feeling that there is only one thing any of my friends would want for this.'

'What?' managed the Squire.

Startup bent over and told him.

'Eeeeeoooow!' shrieked the other and nearly swooned. When he opened his eyes, Startup was still there waiting for his answer and he nodded miserably.

'I'll do what I can,' promised Startup. 'No more.' He walked away sighing and shaking his head at the seemingly enormous problem, looking back once or twice to see if squirrel was watching him, and shaking his head again.

Directly he was out of sight, he collapsed on the ground, rolling over and over with howls of glee. With a bound, he jumped on the nearest tree trunk and placing two fingers in his mouth let out a piercing whistle that echoed around the garden.

Meanwhile, after reporting what he'd just seen to his wife, George received some very odd looks, and it was not until she was persuaded to look out of the window some time later that she began to believe him.

'Look, George, what are all those little animals doing, coming up the path?' she called out excitedly. 'Look, there's some more rabbits, all kinds of birds, and a funny old owl.'

'There's no need to pull my leg about it,' he answered stiffly.

'No, I mean it. See for yourself – quick.'

Much against his will, George allowed himself to be pulled across to the window and glanced out briefly. He shut his eyes and had another look. 'Great galloping gumps,' he blinked. He'd never seen so many animals in his life.

Where had they come from, and what were they doing?

He took another look down at the porch, and received another shock. Each of the animals appeared to be bending over the pile of nuts and picking up as many as they could carry, before heading off down the garden again. He shook his head in disbelief.

'They're helping themselves to the nuts. What on earth do they want with them?'

His wife settled back, and made herself comfortable with a cushion. 'This is fun – much better than watching telly. How many do you think there are?'

George shrugged his shoulders helplessly. 'I've no idea. All I know is they've saved me the problem of getting rid of thousands of nuts. Good luck to them.'

In all the confusion, there was only one person who seemed to know what was going on, and that was Startup. He stood at the foot of the tree where Squire Nabbit was hiding, marking off the score as each animal dropped his or her offering through the hole in the trunk.

'There's another hundred on its way,' he shouted down the hole. 'Mind your head.'

A howl answered him.

'That's another box of lettuces you owe me, Squire,' he called out. To the others, 'Keep it up, lads, you're doing a grand job. Are you counting down there, Squire? That's four hundred and fifty-seven, another sixty. And here's two more bags, and four more coming – don't stop, keep at it.'

What seemed like hours later to the exhausted squirrel waiting down the hole, he heard rabbit call out cheerfully. 'Right, that's most of the load now, Squire. While we're waiting, you might as well start signing these I.O.U's as part of the bargain. Here you are. That one is for Hedgie the Hedgehog – he's just arrived with two dozen spiked nuts. That's him paid off. Off you go, Hedgie. Next, Clara Goose. Silly old Goose, I see you've been spending all your money again. Perhaps this will help you. Off you go.' He checked his tally, and rattled off an endless list of debts run up by the animals all over Hookwood – now paid off in full.

'What would you do without us, Squire?' he winked at Owl. 'Just sign here, here and here. Good, now you can't complain that nobody comes to see you again.'

He waved at the waiting queue and grinned. 'Keep going lads. All this big business is too much for me for one day. I think I'll go and have a rest. Bye for now.' Placed his ear to the trunk, he heard a sleepy voice chanting. 'Four thousand, seven hundred and twenty-one, four thousand seven hundred and twenty-two,'....yawn, 'four thousand, seven hundred and...'

'Any time you want some help with a small insignificant service, Squire, let me know. Goodness,' he added, imitating Squire, 'what a busy life banking is...or should I say...? Never mind.'

With a cheery grin, he took an enormous bite out of a juicy carrot – the first down payment on one of the nuttiest deals he had ever arranged.

Chapter Three

Careless Clara

Young Startup found himself quite a hero when news of his exploits flew around Hookwood. It might have gone to his head, if it had not been for the matter-of-fact way he was greeted when he got back to his burrow.

Dora, his mother, was busily running up curtains, and his father was making new windows and doors for their new home, grumbling as he did so.

'Darned if I see why we need to move,' he was muttering to himself when young Startup looked in.

'Now then,' fretted Dora, coming across them as Ben was getting out his pipe for a quiet smoke. 'There's no time for slacking. We're not staying here another night, there's not even a front door.'

'But what's wrong with where we are?' asked Startup puzzled. 'If we move across to the other bank, we'll be cut off from all our friends.'

'That's exactly what I've been saying,' beamed his father. 'Makes no sense.'

His wife eyed him majestically. 'I know what kind of friends you keep, Benjamin, and I don't care for them.'

He shuffled his feet.

'Besides,' she said with a determined toss of her head. 'We'll be far safer away from that ginger cat – and have a better class of neighbour as well. Now then,' she lifted her paw to stifle any further protest. 'We haven't got all day. Startup, you can give your father a hand while I get on with some proper work. Hold his hammer or something.'

She snatched her husband's pipe out of his mouth, 'And you can give me that for a start, nasty smelly old thing.' Before he could open his mouth in protest, she was marching off with the offending article, holding it out at arm's length.

The absence of his beloved pipe made Ben very snappy, and young Startup did not help matters by dropping the hammer on his father's toes. His father went a shade of purple, and told him to look after the nails instead. Startup found them awkward to hold, and they kept slipping out of his grasp and bounced all over the place. Then his father made it worse by sitting on them by mistake, and nearly hit the roof.

'Go and help your mother, boy,' he howled. 'See if she can put up with you. But not with those nails,' he added hastily. 'I'll have them. Ow!' he yelped, 'not point first.'

Startup mooched off to see what his mother was doing. He was rapidly losing interest in the whole idea of helping people. They didn't appear to appreciate anything he did. After looking around the burrow, his mother didn't seem to be anywhere, so he decided to try his hand at something himself.

At first he had a go at feeding some plaited rushes through the top of the curtains, ready to put them up. But they came undone directly he touched them. In no time at all, he ended up in a terrible mess with bits of rushes sticking out everywhere.

When his mother saw his efforts, she sighed exasperated. 'For goodness sakes, go outside and let me get on with it, or we'll be here until Christmas.' Seeing a spark of hope dawning on his face, she said sharply, 'We're not staying here that long either. Why don't you go and make yourself useful to someone else?'

'But what can I do?' asked Startup, feeling thoroughly bored.

'I'll tell you what you can do,' said his mother struck by a sudden thought, 'you can go and keep an eye on that silly Clara Goose. Now she doesn't have to pay Squire Nabbit all that money she owed him, she'll have all the rogues in the village after her savings. She's so soft, there's no knowing what they might get up to – specially those nasty brown rats, I shouldn't wonder.'

Even the bravest of the rabbit clan were careful to keep a respectable distance from the brown rats, and usually the very mention of their leader, King Freddie, and his crafty friend, Captain Mayfair, was enough to make them scurry for cover.

But Startup was too young to worry about such things, and gladly agreed to his mother's suggestion. He made his way up the sandy bank into the garden with a frisky hop and a skip. It was good to be out and about on such a beautiful day, so he decided to go the long way around to Clara's nest at the bottom of the garden.

The pathway led him down the outside of the hedge, separating the garden from Farmer Smith's field. It was a friendly, well worn path used by many of the animals in Hookwood. It ran past the end of the garden and all the way around the edge of the five acre field, and had been there as long as everyone could remember. It was very handy in an emergency, as a quick retreat if the gamekeeper appeared without warning, as he sometimes did. And if you felt particularly energetic, the path took you on through the churchyard and out overlooking the high street at the old Church lytch gate.

But Startup had no plans for going quite as far as that on such a hot and sunny day. Indeed, he kept on bumping into so many friends on the way, all wanting to congratulate him on outsmarting Squire Nabbit, that he found himself basking in the admiration, and felt in no hurry to go and look for Clara Goose. He leaned back against the old oak tree on the corner and closed his eyes contentedly. It was not until he heard some strange mutterings in the distance that he bothered to straighten up and see who it was.

Shading his eyes against the sun, he peered across the field, and there was Leonard, the Hare, weaving his way towards him in his usual dreamy fashion. Sometimes he would leap in the air for no apparent reason, before stopping suddenly and holding forth to an imaginary audience. Nearby, even Tug, the Robin, forgot he was hunting for a tasty snack and hopped onto a handy branch to watch, while his victim, Spike the worm, arched his back to get a better view.

'Oh, it's only Lenny the Loony,' said Tug, his bright eyes blinking impatiently. 'I haven't got time to listen to that crackpot. Now, what was I doing?' He cocked his head on one side, then he hopped down again, and Spike just had time to slide back before Robin pounced.

Startup came to with a sudden jerk. He had no desire to get caught in a dotty discussion with Hare, and started making his way towards the hedge, hoping to give the impression that he had not noticed him. He was almost there when he glimpsed an agitated figure out of the corner of his eye, bursting through the hedge and fall at Hare's feet. It was Clara Goose.

She immediately launched into a confused babble of squawks, pointing indignantly behind her and quivering all over. 'That horrible man! He's ruined my nest, my beautiful garden – everything. What am I to do?'

Forgetting himself, Startup edged closer, intrigued to hear more. But by the time he was within earshot, Clara had become strangely dumb, hypnotized by Hare's wild staring eyes. After a while however, she recovered and poured out her woes all over again.

'He's thrown everything into the pond – all my belongings and treasured possessions. But I see you understand, dear Leonard. Will you help me? I'm a poor little goose, all on my own.'

'My dear lady, fear not,' was Hare's lofty answer. 'While I am here, no one will harm you. Rely on me...' and he puffed out his chest to demonstrate his fitness for the task.

He was about to say more, when his flow of eloquence was slopped in full flight by Startup, who decided to get rid of the scrounger by pointing past him with a quivering paw.

'What is it?' asked Hare sharply.

'Would – would that be ... Farmer Smith's gamekeeper?' pretended Startup with a gulp.

'Where...?' Leonard the Hare shivered, swinging around in an agitated manner. Without pausing, he bounded a few feet away and called back. 'Can't stop...just remembered...awfully pressing engagement, dear lady. I shall be back, never fear...'

Tears started welling up in Clara's eyes. 'I thought you said you would help me...'

'Bang,' said Startup simply. The sooner Lenny the Loony was away, the better, he decided. Hare was the sort of animal that would be after her money in no time. He looked so pathetic that old ladies were always pressing money on him, and Startup saw no reason why Clara should fall for that. Hare was not to be trusted where silly geese were concerned.

He needn't have worried. Fancying he heard a gun going off, Hare leaped another few feet in the air and his voice grew fainter as he hurried off. 'Don't worry, dear lady. I won't forget. Rely on me.'

'Oh, bother the hare,' gasped Clara, choked with self pity. She looked suspiciously at Startup. 'I thought you said the gamekeeper was coming.'

'Oh, did I?' the young rabbit replied innocently. 'I was only asking myself a question...like you would say, have you seen Mr Fox lately?'

Clara gathered her shawl around her uneasily. 'What nonsense you do talk. Here am I beset with troubles, and all you do is make fun of me.' Her voice trembled, and she tried fluttering her eyelashes at him.

Thinking she might have something in her eye, Startup fished out a rather grubby handkerchief and offered it to her.

Clara drew back offended, but the thought of her predicament started her croaking again, and she flapped her wings so much she nearly overbalanced.

'Go away, young rabbit, if that's all you have to offer. You're no help at all,' she sniffed. Then added, 'Rabbits have nasty habits, I always did say.'

Startup gave up. There was a limit to what a young rabbit could do. He pottered around the garden for a while, nibbling at a few carrots, and eventually came across Clara's nest – or what was left of it. At one time, it must have looked a charming sight, built as it was in the middle of a pond and surrounded by tall wavy trees. But over the years, without anyone to look after it, the pond had become overgrown and matted.

As he gazed around rather bewildered, the whole area looked as if it a whirlwind had struck it. Someone, he realised, must have tried to clear it up, and in doing so had swept all of Clara's belongings to one side. All that remained of her nest were a few broken sticks, and the rest of her things were spread all over the grass. It would take ages for anyone to sort that lot out, he whistled. But being a kind young rabbit, he began to pick up an odd piece here and there, more as a gesture than anything else. It was a hopeless task, and he was about to give up when a clod of earth caught him behind his ear.

Zonk. Before he could react, there was a frantic whirring noise and he found himself being beaten around his head. He looked up astonished, and saw Clara shrieking at him.

'So, it was you, you horrible little rabbit. I might have known.'

'Here, steady on...' Startup did his best to calm her down, but Clara refused to listen.

'And all the time I thought it was that beastly man up at the cottage – and it was really you. Wait till I get at you!'

Startup took one look at her wings spread out as she advanced towards him, and had second thoughts. This was not the scatter-brained Clara he thought he knew – it was a new and totally transformed goose, defending what was left of her home the only way she knew. With a quick hop and a skip, he put the trees between them, and then he was running as fast as he could, with the sound of Clara crashing through the undergrowth behind him, bent on revenge.

Being fleet of foot, Startup luckily soon outdistanced the clumsy goose, who was more at home in the water. At last feeling safe from pursuit, he paused to get his breath back and nibbled a few lettuce heads while he thought out what to do next.

Looking after Clara, he considered, was not quite as easy as he had imagined. Used to making quick decisions, he was beginning to realise that some animals – particularly certain unmentionable geese - did not see things the same way. Tomorrow, he thought hopefully, she might feel differently, and with that optimistic notion uppermost in his mind, he went home.

Up in the house, George had a similar untroubled mind. He always tried to maintain a simple outlook on life, and did not intend to overtax his brains unduly. So when he told his wife with a certain measure of satisfaction that he has cleared up that disgusting mess down at the pond, he was surprised and a little hurt at her response.

'Oh, no, George,' she cried horrified. 'Not that poor goose's nest – what will she do? She's got nowhere to go. How could you?'

And she went on about it at such a great length that George got quite confused and had to have a stiff drink to recover. Unfortunately, the choice was rather limited, and as he sat there nursing his cocoa, his head grew quite dizzy grappling with the problem.

Luckily, he didn't have to worry about it for too long because the solution came quickly to Joan. 'You'll just have to put it all back again,' and she dismissed the matter from her mind. She had more pressing decisions to make that demanded her attention, like what they were going to have for supper.

'Right then,' he sighed with relief, and with the weight lifted from his mind he took a final swig of his cocoa, forgetting what it was and nearly choked.

Next morning, he crept down the garden as soon as it was light, and set about putting it all back as he remembered it. He was so successful that when Clara called back to collect her tattered belongings, she felt almost at home again.

After a few sniffs, she felt perhaps she had been a little unkind to young Startup, since he appeared to make a good job of it, and decided to make amends. She set off immediately to look for him, and eventually came across a trail of carrot tops. Following them up, she found him stuffing himself to gain some courage, ready to face another day of doing good deeds.

'Ah, there you are rabbit. About that misunderstanding yesterday...'

At the sound of her voice, he started and nearly swallowed a carrot the wrong way...'Misunderstanding?' he got out at last.

'I've decided to forget all about yesterday,' she announced grandly. 'Rabbits will be rabbits, I suppose, although they do have funny habits. Now let's dismiss it from our minds.' She spread herself, preening her feathers. 'There am I prattling on, and I promised to meet Hare for a walk, down by the river.'

'But that's where the brown rats live,' said Startup anxiously. 'Don't go down there.'

'Oh, I shan't worry,' she tossed her head. 'Leonard will look after me – he fears nothing, you know.'

'But you mustn't. It isn't safe.'

'Come, come,' she fluttered her lashes as she waddled off. 'Or I shall think you're jealous of him.'

'Golly,' stuttered Startup, watching her leave. 'What am I going to do now?'

Not wanting her to get the wrong idea, he set off slowly, keeping her just in sight over the top of the grass. Every now and then, Clara would stop and look back to see if she was being followed, and Startup had to duck down out of sight behind the nearest clump of grass. Unfortunately, some of the clumps were full of nasty thistles and nettles, and he soon got fed up with it.

'Females,' he kept mumbling to himself, and it was only the thought of the promise he'd made to his mother that kept him going.

Soon Clara decided there were more uplifting thoughts than stupid rabbits that pulled her home to pieces, and she began to dream about her brave hare. After that, she stopped looking around, and Startup began to get more and more confident, and before long he became so reckless he did not even look where he was going.

It was a great mistake. The next time he came to a ditch, he jumped across without thinking and landed on something sharp. Unfortunately, it turned out to be the prongs of a rake that one of the farm hands had left behind. Before he had time to react, the handle whizzed up and hit him with a whack, and he staggered around in circles, before keeling over in a blaze of coloured stars.

It seemed hours later when he finally managed to get up and pull himself together. At first, he thought he saw a row of owls peering at him through a mist. He put up a paw to steady himself, and the heads swung up and down, and split into half a dozen rows, all wheeling and spinning around. After a while, they merged into one row, then the eight heads became four, then two and at last he was able to recognise the familiar face of Grumps, the old owl, who was hopping impatiently from one leg to the other.

'Been at the nettle wine again, eh?'

Startup grabbed hold of him. 'Where is she?'

'Where's who?' said Grumps, turning his head sideways and regarding him oddly with his one good eye.

'Clara, of course,' groaned Startup.

'You mean, Clara the goose?' rebuked Grumps in surprise. 'You're far too young for all that nonsense. Anyway, she's ugly as sin - even I can see that.'

Startup started to explain, and as he did so the disbelieving look faded from Grumps eyes.

'Down by the river, you say? What's she doing there?'

The sun was now high in the sky, and Startup was worried about how long he had been knocked out as he gabbled out his story.

'If only my good-for-nothing nephews were here,' fretted Grumps, as he listened. 'Goodness knows what those dratted brown rats are getting up to down there – they need teaching a sharp lesson.' He glanced down towards the river. 'Trouble is I'm getting too old for this sort of nonsense. I'm no use in a fight any more.'

Startup's eyes opened in surprise. He'd never heard the owl talk like that before. 'I didn't ask for any help,' he started to apologise, which only made it worse.

'So, I'm not good enough for you, eh? Well, I'll be off. Fight the rats yourself and see where that gets you. I don't care.' The old owl stood there trembling.

'I didn't mean anything, honest, Grumps,' pleaded Startup. 'Only I have to get help. If you could let the others know...' he added hopefully.

'Get on with you young fellow,' growled Grumps. 'I'll get them rounded up, see if I don't.'

He watched Startup out of sight, and made a determined effort to fly for assistance. It was obvious from the awkward way he limped, he was in no great shape. After a few hops, he managed with a struggle to get off the ground and flapped his wings, swooping in short bursts. After zigzagging across the field, he finally flopped at the feet of Oswald the Duck, who was wandering around aimlessly.

'Get help for Startup...brown rats at the river bank...' he managed, before collapsing in a heap.

Oswald looked down at him vacantly and scratched himself. It was a hard life for a duck to understand what was going on.

Sometimes he thought it was too much for him. He leaned over and pecked at Grumps.

'Quack,' he uttered thoughtfully, and waddled off with a frown.

Meanwhile, Startup was imagining all kinds of things that might be happening to Clara, as he hurried to the river bank. Visions of her being tied up and bullied were flashing through his mind, and made him so worried he literally bounced along.

By the time he crawled the last twenty yards or so to reach the rats HQ without being seen, he was expecting the worst. When he cautiously peeped into the nearest bunker, he was astonished to see that Clara and Leonard were chatting to one of the brown rats as if it were just a social call. He blinked. This was no ordinary rat, he realised. Unless his eyes deceived him, the rat was wearing a fawn waistcoat and wore a monocle.

Clara was prattling on. '...to cap it all, after pulling down my house, that impudent rabbit tried to stop me coming to see you.'

'No,' cried Leonard and the brown rat together, in mock outrage.

The silly goose fluttered her eyelashes. 'Of course, I told him I had my brave Hare to look after me.'

Leonard looked suitable modest, and the brown rat slapped him on the back.

'Bravo, my dear chap.' He spoke in a funny fluted kind of voice, and looked far superior to any other rat Startup had ever seen.

A hard hat, he thought grimly.

'There are some very nasty villains about,' the brown rat sighed piously, 'can't trust anyone these days, eh Hare?'

Hare caught on. 'Captain Mayfair is quite right, dear lady.' He shook his head sadly, 'there are always people about who are after something that doesn't belong to them.'

There was a nasty snigger in the background, and the brown rat coughed to cover the noise.

'To be absolutely honest,' said Leonard hastily, 'we were more than a little suspicious about that young rabbit they call Startup, weren't we, Captain?'

'Absolutely, my dear chap,' agreed the Captain smoothly. 'And we were thinking you ought to be a little more careful about your savings, where that greedy young rabbit is concerned.'

Startup listened with growing indignation.

'Really?' said Clara, a little bewildered.

Gaining confidence, Hare plunged on. 'Captain Mayfair was saying only just before you came, how much we could help you, dear lady.'

'But Leonard,' squeaked Clara, 'with you to guard me, nobody could possibly steal my nest egg.'

'Well, I won't always be here to look after you,' said Hare soulfully.

Clara's eyes opened in fright, and started filling with tears. 'You're not going to desert me, are you, Leonard?'

'Of course he isn't,' interrupted the Captain quickly. 'But he does get called away on important business, from time to time, isn't that what you meant, Hare?'

'Er, yes,' said Hare gratefully. 'Now we were thinking, Clara – if I may call you that...'

'Oh, but of course, Leonard,' said Clara coyly.

Hare gulped and plunged in. 'You see, our idea is that you could give your money to...er...' he searched around for a suitable phrase, and Clara's adoring look began to fade.

'...to us to invest,' hissed the Captain, out of the corner of his mouth.

Mishearing, Hare panicked. '...so that the Captain can keep it in his vest...'

Captain Mayfair closed his eyes in prayer, and pushed Hare aside with a pained expression. 'Madam, let me tell you of my vision.'

'Your...what?' repeated Clara, intrigued in spite of herself.

'In a nutshell....peace of mind,' the Captain cried dramatically. 'Tell me lady, wouldn't you like to own your own piece of land, all your own, that nobody would be able to tear down again?'

'Oh, yes, I would,' agreed Clara with feeling.

'Well,' the Captain paused impressively. 'I can promise you that right away. It's yours.'

'Oh, good,' accepted Clara in a matter-of-fact voice. 'When can I move in?'

Hare moaned quietly, but the Captain continued as if he hadn't heard. He got so excited, his voice lost its fluty polish and sounded slightly foreign. 'Ve shall get it for you, never fear. But first we need your help...to fight for our rights...so we can drive out the wicked imperialists and reactionaries...'

'What's he talking about?' whispered Clara.

'Landowners,' muttered Hare, rather embarrassed.

Captain Mayfair broke off, as he noticed her interest waning. 'What I'm trying to say, dear lady, is that we will look after it for you, and it will earn you much interest...'

Clara's eyes gleamed. 'How much?'

'As much as you want,' assured the Captain blandly. 'You will be rich and famous, and own plenty of land. Now, can we be assured of your support?'

Hare saw her hesitate and whispered. 'He means, when can we have our money, dear Clara? I look into the future, and see that we will be drawn together closer than ever in this great scheme...just you and me.'

Clara's heart gave a great bound. His words sounded like heavenly music. The sight of his soft brown eyes gazed at her beseechingly made her head swoon.

'Don't look now,' she said coyly, and turned away to pull out her purse dangling inside her collar.

Startup watched in dismay as the Captain and Hare edged a little closer, waiting to pounce.

Without thinking, Startup yelled, 'look out, Clara!'

There was immediate pandemonium. Hare snatched his hand back guiltily, and the Captain called out furiously. 'Guard, seize him!'

Startup looked around quickly. His words seemed to have stirred up a hornet's nest. Within seconds, he was startled to see a horde of snarling rats pouring out of the ground. There was only one thing for it. He threw a leg over the edge of the bunker and with a bound made a dive for the money before they could get their hands on it. He saw Clara standing there uncertainly, her mouth wide open. In the confusion, Captain Mayfair was stealthily cutting through the cords holding the purse, and was about to snatch it when Startup came to the rescue.

He grabbed at Clara and pulled her away. To his surprise, Clara resisted and flung her shawl at him crying, 'Stop thief!' Hardly able to see with the shawl wrapped around his head, Startup ploughed on. He might have got away with it if it hadn't been for Hare craftily putting out his long back foot to trip him up. By the time Startup managed to get up, he was immediately set upon by a gang of brown rats and held fast.

'So,' the Captain said slowly, 'you are the rabbit we were talking about? Young Startup, they call you, hein? Well, let me tell you something, rabbit. You will not be starting anything anymore. You understand?'

Startup flinched at the words, but tried not to show it. 'You won't get away with it,' he said bravely.

The Captain did not bother to answer. He was checking the contents of the purse. Satisfied, he threw it to Hare who took care not to look at Clara as he stuffed it in his pocket.

Turning at last to his prisoner, the Captain smiled contemptuously.

'This is only the start. Very soon now we will have enough for our cause, and then you will see, eh Hare?'

Leonard nodded uncomfortably.

'Meanwhile,' mused the Captain, 'we must arrange a suitable accident for you and...' he bowed to Clara, 'your charming companion.'

Startup tried to bargain, while Clara stood there looking forlorn. 'Look, let her go and nobody will ever know...'

The Captain's reply was blunt and to the point. 'We no longer have any need for your help, dear lady. A pity, when we were just beginning to enjoy your company.' He nodded his dismissal at Leonard who scuttled thankfully for the exit.

'Leonard, don't leave me...' cried Clara piteously. But Leonard was already out of sight.

The Captain took one last look. 'I must go as well. Farewell, dear lady...'

Left alone, Clara burst out unexpectedly. 'It was all your fault, Rabbit. If you hadn't tried to steal my purse, none of this would have happened.'

Startup gazed at her speechlessly. 'Me...?' he stuttered, but she wouldn't let him get a word in.

'It's typical of a rabbit. No consideration,' she wailed bitterly. 'Look what you did to Leonard – he was so ashamed, he had to leave.'

Startup struggled to speak, but a squealing band of rats surrounded them and hustled them out.

At the river bank, a lean brown rat expertly tied their hands together, and the other end of the rope was wound around a large rock.

Hearing a sudden whirring noise overhead, Startup looked up hopefully. The rat smirked, 'You'll need more than wings where you're going,' and nodded to the others waiting eagerly.

Startup was jostled nearer to the river's edge, and it only seemed a matter of minutes before it was all over. Just then, a dark shadow seemed to black out the sky, and the rats fell back panic stricken.

Out of the sky swooped what appeared to be hundreds of flashing shapes, darting to and fro, then diving straight at the milling rats, and chasing them away amid shrill cries and curses.

Soon afterwards, Startup felt one of them attacking the ropes holding him, then they fell away and he found he was free. Overjoyed, he tried to thank his rescuers who turned out to be one of Grumps nephews.

The young owl looked around and panted. 'Don't hang around. Just tell Uncle we got here in time, or we'll never hear the last of it – I'm off.'

'Why, what's wrong?' asked Startup puzzled.

But the owl was up and away fast. 'Because there's only three of us, that's why,' he hooted, 'and the others have gone already...'

Startup rolled over and over, laughing at the way the brown rats had been fooled. Elated at his narrow escape, he looked around for Clara, but found she was already strutting off up the path, her head held high.

The rabbit grinned and followed her. Catching up, he pulled out a familiar shape and held it up for the goose to see.

She squawked, 'My purse! Where did you find it?'

Startup gazed modestly at the ground. 'Leonard was so anxious to get away, he didn't notice me slipping it out of his pocket.'

Clara bridled and snatched at it. 'He was only looking after it for me,' she sniffed.

Startup scratched his head in disbelief and watched her waddle away, full of her own importance. Before turning the corner, she fell back on her parting shot. 'I always did say that rabbits have nasty habits.' And with that she was gone.

Chapter Four

First move

Startup wasted no time in searching out Grumps to thank him. He found the old owl propped up in bed, looking pale and tired, being fussed over by his sister, Letty.

'I hear those lazy nephews of mine managed it then,' he grunted, tugging weakly at the sheets, while his sister was patiently smoothing them out to make him look tidy. He was only a shadow of his former self, the rabbit noted anxiously. Startup thanked the old owl awkwardly, before telling him about his adventures.

Soon old Grumps forgot all about his health as he tried to puzzle out the strange behaviour of Leonard the Hare and the villainous brown rats.

Hare, he dismissed as lazy and plain foolish, but, 'that brown rat - Captain Mayfair, as they call him - he sounds a real danger, and no mistake.' Old Grumps hesitated, 'I don't usually pass on tittle tattle before I've had a chance to check it out, but I did hear that he's been sent in to stir up trouble – and what you say about him only bears that out.'

'What sort of trouble?' asked Startup curiously, as he watched the owl fixed in gloomy thought.

'You heard what he said,' snapped old Owl with some of his former fire. 'He's looking for idiots to hand over their hard earned money so that he can mastermind a revolution and have hordes of brown rats taking over our countryside.' He drew himself up and thundered, 'I'd rather die first!'

Suiting action to words, he fell back on his pillows and closed his eyes with such conviction, Startup thought that he had.

Drawing near, Startup bent over to listen to Owl's breathing and as he did so, old Grumps suddenly opened one eye and glared up at him.

'I'm not dead yet, young rabbit.' Then his voice softened as he regarded the worried face in front of him. 'You think I'm an old fusspot, don't you?'

As Startup vigorously shook his head, the owl said sombrely, 'You mark my words, that brown rat wants watching. When I'm better, I'm going to get me my telescope, and keep a watch on them vermin down by the river from my vantage point at the top of the tree...'

As his sister made protesting noises in the background, he grinned unexpectedly and said, 'that will be part of my resting up plan to get better, Letty. Finest vantage point for miles is my oak tree, I promise you. Now,' he nodded at Startup, 'that'll be my job over the next few weeks - it's all I can do in my state. It's up to you now, young rabbit. Get out and tell all our animal friends about the danger. We must band together and fight,' he warned, 'if we want to keep our countryside free...,' before collapsing in a fit of coughing.

While Startup was still working out how he was going to carry out the task all by himself, he was briskly shooed out of the room by Letty, who immediately rushed back to see to her brother.

Obediently, Startup went around looking up all his neighbours, and told them about his encounter with Clara Goose, and about rescuing her savings from the clutches of Hare and Captain Mayfair. At first, they thought he was pulling their legs, knowing his fondness for practical jokes. And as he listened to himself telling the same story over and over again and watching their faces, the young rabbit couldn't help admitting to himself it sounded a tall story.

After a while however, the animals grew tired of hearing the same old story, and began to get a little short with him, some even slamming the door in his face. It reminded him of the time he was canvassing votes for the rabbit council.

In desperation, he called on Clara and asked her to back up his story, but received a very frosty reception. The reason became all too clear the next morning when Clara paraded down Tanfield High Street, coyly showing off a flashing ring, and dragging the modest figure of Leonard the Hare along behind her.

Startup stared after her, hardly able to believe his eyes, for the silly goose was gaily announcing her engagement, to anyone who showed the slightest interest, and to a great many others who didn't and weren't. Moreover, Hare was periodically dipping his hand into a large bag and handing out...wads of money. Startup blinked in amazement. Where could it have all come from?

In a flash, the news was around Hookwood, and the animals ran out to tell Startup what they thought about his latest leg pull. Some were good natured about it, but others were quite indignant, and one or two threw things at him for trying to upset the 'poor girl'.

'You ought to be ashamed of yourself, young rabbit,' boomed Squire Nabbit pompously, wagging a finger at him.

Startup felt quite bewildered. These were the very same neighbours who had gone out of their way to congratulate him for getting their money back from that chiselling moneylender – and now to be lectured by the rogue himself was the last straw.

Feeling dejected, he decided to go home, and for once in his life he took all the back pathways, to avoid meeting anyone on the way. Pausing, as he found himself at the oak tree, he hesitated for a moment then with a heavy heart he knocked on the door and went inside to report to old Grumps.

To his surprise, Owl received the news quite calmly.

'Shrewd, very shrewd,' he commented in what Startup could only describe later as a note of admiration. 'Don't you see, we've got them worried,' he said excitedly. 'The cunning devils. That money bag was a touch of genius. They'll never believe you now.'

'That's what I've been trying to tell you,' groaned Startup.

'Well now, young rabbit,' said Grumps thoughtfully. 'This is not quite the challenge you expected, eh?'

Startup nodded his head vigorously. 'You could say that again. What am I going to do?'

Owl struggled to his feet. 'Why this is an opportunity to find out who your friends really are,' he said triumphantly. 'Tell you what – let's have a Council of War. You go and round them up. Hurry up, I'm beginning to feel better all ready.'

'I wish I were,' said Startup sadly.

He went out counting off his friends one by one, and the more he thought about it, the shorter the list became.

'Well, this shouldn't take long,' he concluded gloomily, 'my name must be mud by now.' After mooching around he came across his friend, Puggles the Pig, nosing around in thick black mud in his sty.

'Hail, young rabbit,' Puggles acknowledged his greeting. 'Tell me, why is it that mud is supposed to be good for the skin? I spend half my life in the wretched stuff, and it doesn't seem to do me any good.'

'Yes, yes,' said Startup hurriedly, knowing how much Puggles loved talking about his looks. 'This is important, Puggles - it's about Clara.'

'Hmm,' pondered his friend. 'There's another one who could do with some treatment. She'll never get married with a face like that.'

'Ah,' said Startup, grateful for the cue. 'That's where you're wrong,' and proceeded to tell his friend all about it, as well as the latest turn of events.

Puggles thought deeply for a moment, then said cordially, 'Crumbs old lad, you are in a bit of a rabbit's stew this time, aren't you?' He snorted once or twice with the effort of concentrating, then announced brightly, 'I know, why don't we ask old Hedgie around for a pow wow - that old Grumps has got something there, you know. And what about Prudence?' he beamed, 'She's a woman, isn't she?'

Startup wasn't sure how this would help, but he had to agree that his cousin, Prudence, did have some good ideas from time to time, and Hedgie, well he was just, Hedgie. Any ideas were worth listening to at this stage.

Prudence arrived ten minutes ahead of Hedgie. 'What's up?' she asked, not wasting any time.

Puggles nodded approvingly. That was a good start. More to follow, he told himself.

Startup plunged into the tale again, while Prudence listened very patiently. 'I think we ought to talk it over with old Grumps,' she said at last. 'He's a wise old owl, and we need someone like him to help us against those horrid brown rats. Ugh,' she shivered, 'I don't like the sound of it. They mean business this time, I'm sure.'

'What a capital idea,' boomed Puggles. 'All we need now is Hedgie. I suppose we'll have to tell him all over again, when he does decide to arrive.'

A voice murmured sleepily from behind a cabbage leaf. 'I heard every word you said.'

'Come on, Hedgie,' cried Startup, brightening up. 'We've been waiting for you.'

Into view rolled a bundle of prickly spikes.

'No need to hurry,' the hedgehog unrolled slowly. 'It'll all be the same tomorrow.'

'What sort of talk is that?' thundered Startup. 'I promised Grumps we'd have a meeting, and sort out something. What am I going to tell him?'

Prudence spoke up firmly. 'He's right, you know, Startup. Grumps sounds as if he's going to need a good night's rest if he's going to get any better. Why don't we sleep on it, and meet at the oak tree after breakfast?'

'Good idea, young Prudence,' echoed Puggles. 'I need a good night's sleep myself, coming to that. Plays havoc with my looks, all this trotting around.'

'Right,' accepted Startup reluctantly. 'I suppose that makes sense. Don't forget then, tomorrow it is, at the oak tree - at nine sharp.' And with a quick flip of his tail, he bounded off, much relieved to his burrow.

'All that wasted time,' grumbled Hedgie. 'Now I'll have to go all the way back round that bush again. It'll take hours.'

'Bye, boys,' smiled Prudence.

With a snort, Hedgie started off on his epic journey once again, and Puggles returned to his sty, and gazed earnestly into a puddle to see if the mud had improved his looks in any way.

The next day turned out to be a beautiful one. It was unusually hot, and the steady drone of the bees wafting down into the burrow made Startup feel very drowsy. But the thought of trying to explain everything to his mother after she had told him to look after Clara, got him out of bed and out of the burrow quicker than anything. Outside, the sun shone, the birds were singing and Startup felt uplifted by the sheer excitement of being part of it all. That is, until he bumped into some of his neighbours.

Being a friendly little rabbit, Startup gave his usual whoop. 'Hey there, how's things?'

'Good morning,' they inclined their heads frostily. It was all a repeat of last night. By the time he arrived at the oak tree his spirits had dropped to zero, and he was beginning to get madder and madder at the injustice of the situation.

'... and another thing!' he burst out at his somewhat startled friends who were waiting for him. 'I don't see why I should be blamed for it.'

'Now then, don't let it get you down,' Prudence tried to calm his spirits. 'We're right behind you, aren't we, boys?'

'Rather,' boomed Puggles, and Hedgie joined in sleepily.

But Startup was not listening. He was gazing straight past them at three figures who were approaching.

Leading the way, was Clara the goose, looking frightfully smug, as she bowed left and right in regal style, while hanging on to Leonard to make sure he did not have second thoughts and slip away.

However, Startup completely forgot about Clara and her problems at that moment, or Leonard come to that. It was the slinky looking figure swaying alongside them that attracted his attention.

Clara deliberately ignored Startup and called out to the others roguishly, 'Hello, have you heard the good news? Leonard and I are getting married.' She might have saved her breath, for all the good it did her. Noticing the complete lack of interest, she turned to see where all the goggled looks were being directed and reluctantly introduced her companion with a casual wave.

'Oh, you haven't met my friend, Lola, have you? She's been staying with those charming brown rats on the river bank.'

'I say, steady on, Hedgie,' cautioned Puggles, as his friend suddenly woke up, and started making some excited grunts and inching forward.

'Hello there,' a purring voice announced itself, and Startup realised with a shock that it was aimed at himself. His knees buckled, and he found himself talking in a strange squeaky voice quite unlike his own.

'Hi! My name's Startup. I er...' He stared hypnotized, as she glided towards him.

'I've heard all about you...' she drawled.

'You have?' he somehow got out, an octave higher than usual.

'Yes,' she murmured. 'That nice Captain Mayfair told me all about you. He likes you.'

'He does?' repeated Startup, quite mystified.

'Startup,' broke in Prudence, quite anxious. 'He's a brown rat. You know you can't trust him.' She was about to add, how can you possibly trust this rabbit when you don't know her, but she kept silent. She could see by the look on his face that it wouldn't be the right moment to voice her suspicions.

Lola reached out and started pulling him away from his friends, and butterflies began a furious dance up and down his spine.

'I have a message for you,' she breathed into his ear. 'Let's go somewhere where we can talk, without anyone bothering us.'

Seeing that he was about to follow her without hesitation, Puggles hooted in a rather cross voice, 'Kindly remember we're your friends as well.'

'Quite right,' echoed Hedgie, 'We're here to help you - Prudence too.'

'Come on,' urged Lola in a soft persuasive voice. 'I've got so many things to tell you...'

'You have?' Startup found himself moving after her, with a silly fixed grin.

'Stop repeating yourself, rabbit. You sound ridiculous,' barked Puggles.

'He sounds like a real sweetie to me,' murmured the young siren.

'We've got a lot to talk about,' croaked Startup weakly, as he found himself in a surprisingly strong grip.

His friends watched in silence.

'You know,' they heard her confide, 'those poor brown rats are so misunderstood — if only you knew them as well as I do...'

'Well...' breathed Prudence at last, after they had gone, 'what do you make of that?'

'Oh, Puggles,' warbled Hedgie, imitating Lola's voice, 'Those poor brown rats are so misunderstood.' He grunted, 'Pah, it makes you sick. I don't know what she's up to, but he's completely besotted. You wouldn't catch me being caught by a woman like that.'

Prudence smiled, relieving the tension. 'She'd have a job with all your prickles, Hedgie.'

'No, we can't all be handsome,' agreed Puggles, admiring himself in a puddle.

Hedgie snorted. 'I know a fake when I see one. I tell you something – she's sounds well in with those brown rats. I bet they put her up to it.'

'Well, she can't fool me,' dismissed Puggles loftily, spoiling the effect by scratching his ear.

'No, but she's doing pretty well with poor old Startup,' sighed Prudence. But if she felt jealous, she didn't intend to show it. 'I think that...Lola' - she said the name with some distaste - 'has other plans for poor old Startup. She was steering him in the direction of the five acre field.'

'Why do they want to go that far?' cried Hedgie, still panting with the effort of climbing up all those stairs.

Prudence gazed anxiously at Grumps, half expecting him to confirm her worst fears.

He hunched up in his bed, looking like a general working out his enemy's next move. 'Let me see,' he traced a route on the squares of the eiderdown in front of him. 'That would take him either round the path to the village, or down the field...' he looked up at Prudence keenly.

She raised her eyebrows gravely, and finished the sentence. '...to the river bank...where the brown rats live.'

They looked at each other blankly.

'I say, old thing, you're absolutely right. We've got to get after them,' spluttered Puggles, lumbering to his feet.

'I'll go,' volunteered Hedgie.

'We haven't got all night,' said Puggles, without thinking.

'No, Hedgie,' said Prudence kindly. 'You've only just got here.'

But Hedgie was hurt and retired into the corner sulking. Prudence sighed and turned to her friend hopefully. 'Puggles?'

'Right-ho, my dear,' agreed Puggles willingly, 'but I'll never catch up in time with my weight. You really need someone a bit faster.'

With a sinking feeling, Prudence caught Grumps looking at her expectantly. 'No, I couldn't possibly spy on Startup,' she protested. 'He's my friend.'

'If you don't go after them,' warned the wise old owl, 'we may be too late.'

The young rabbit gulped and turned to the door without another word.

'In the meantime, you two...,' Grumps pulled away his bedclothes with an effort, '...can help me up to my telescope. We must find out what's going on.'

Prudence hurried across the garden as fast as her legs would carry her.

When she reached the hedge that bordered the five acre field, she peered anxiously up and down the path for a sign of her friend, without success.

It was a large field, and halfway across it dipped into a fold before continuing down to the river.

At the thought of where he might be going – right into a trap set by that villainous Captain Mayfair and his ferocious band of brown rats – her blood froze.

'I must try to save him,' she gasped. All caution gone, she ran straight across the field, taking the shortest route she knew that would lead her to the rats HQ.

While she was worrying, the object of her concern was stepping blithely through the long grass just over the brow of the hill, humming gaily to himself. He was so busy drinking in the admiring glances of his companion, the lovely Lola, that he did not once stop to think where he was, or where he was going.

'I say, isn't it a beautiful day, Cousin Lola, and what an extraordinary coincidence, you finding out we're related.'

'Mm,' she said dreamily. 'Makes you feel we belong together somehow.'

'I've never known such a super day,' burbled Startup.' The sun's shining, the birds are singing...' He broke off, 'At least, the birds were singing just a minute ago. That's funny, I wonder why it's gone so quiet.'

'I expect they thought we wanted to be alone,' she whispered coyly, hastily waving a slinking figure out of sight.

'That's funny,' repeated Startup innocently. 'Everything seems to have gone dark, all of a sudden – even the grass looks kind of... brown.'

Lola clutched his paw tightly. 'I expect the farmer's been burning off the stubble,' she remarked brightly.

'But it's too tall for that... and look, it's moving.' Startup shook his head and looked away, thinking he was seeing things. Then he froze, suddenly aware of a long line of rats creeping up on him, not more than a dozen yards away.

'Why don't you close your eyes?' Lola leaned over to cover his face with her scarf. 'My friends are getting ready a lovely surprise.' She may have thought Startup believed her, but there were others with different ideas on the subject.

Unbeknown to either of them, their actions were being observed from an upstairs window in Oak Tree cottage, perched high above them.

'Here,' cried George with dawning interest as he caught sight of them. 'There's that wretched rabbit. I'll have him this time.'

'Yes, dear,' soothed his wife. 'Just as you say.'

Then she noticed him picking up his shotgun which, now it was repaired, looked even more dangerous than ever. She called out nervously, 'Not in the house, George!'

Caught up in the excitement, George took no notice and swung the gun around, loading it clumsily at the same time.

'George!' she shrieked, 'not with the window shut!'

Appalled, she reached out to stop him, but only managed to jolt his arm as he fired.

The shot fortunately missed Startup completely, but the terrible noise the shotgun made and the piercing screams that rent the air as Joan saw the window disappear in front of her, had a devastating effect on the army of rats laying in wait below. To George's bemused eyes, the field became alive with masses of brown shapes, twisting and turning in their frantic efforts to escape.

'Look at that!' he whooped, blazing away. 'The field is full of bally rats. Tallyho!'

It was a sight that had Puggles and Hedgie yelling with delight, and even Grumps was beaming as they espied the glorious scene from the top of the old oak tree.

As far as Prudence was concerned, it seemed like a miraculous intervention. She darted in and grabbed hold of Startup who was standing there with a slightly dazed look on his face.

'No, you don't,' she said happily and trod hard on Lola's foot. Yelping, the young spy let go and took off after the fleeing rats.

Chapter Five

Down by the river

Fred the postman wheeled his bicycle slowly up the lane, stopping every now and then to mop his brow with a large and colourful handkerchief

He was so busy doing this that he almost passed the stone steps leading up to Oak Tree Cottage before he realised where he was. With a sigh of relief, he propped his old trusty two-wheeler against the bank, and sat down for a few minutes.

'Well now,' he rummaged in his post bag, 'what have I got for Oak Tree today? No bills, I 'opes.'

Just then there was a lollopy sort of sound, and down the steps came or rather drifted a dreamy looking Startup.

'Hold up, if it isn't that frisky young rabbit,' hailed Fred.

If Startup saw him he gave no sign, and sat down a short distance away, staring into the distance.

'I see, like that, is it?' grunted Fred. 'I know how you feel chum, and I've only just started.'

He fished an envelope out of his pocket and held it up to the light. 'Now, what have we got? Oh, only a bill for the young gent. They won't like that when they've just moved in.'

Scratching his head, he glanced at Startup. 'Which reminds me, I don't know whether you've noticed, my young friend, but there's a heck of a lot of rats down the lane. And they're chock a block on the river. I would watch it, if I were you.'

Giving up at the lack of response, he clambered ponderously to his feet. 'Well, don't say I didn't warn you. I can't stay here gossiping all day, must get on.'

As he went by, there was a rustle in the grass and Prudence emerged followed by old Ben, busily puffing his pipe.

'Oh, there you are, Startup,' she cried thankfully. 'We were getting quite worried about you disappearing like that, after all that trouble with the brown rats.'

Startup looked up vaguely. 'Trouble, what trouble? I didn't see any when I was down in the field with Lola yesterday.'

Prudence shook her head patiently. 'That was three days ago, you chump.'

Old Ben drew hard on his pipe and choked. 'While you've been mooning around, the rats have been getting up to all kinds of mischief. Didn't you hear what the postman said? They're all over the bottom of the lane, and getting up to no good on the river, by all accounts.'

A trusting look spread over Startup's face. 'Lola says the brown rats are our friends.'

Ben spluttered at the thought. 'She's just leading you up the garden, my lad, and you're a fool if you can't see it. But don't listen to me...'

A majestic voice called down. 'Ben!'

At the unmistakeable tones of his wife Dora, Ben scuttled off muttering. 'Nobody listens to me.'

Prudence eyed Startup with friendly exasperation. 'What has Lola done to you?'

'I wish I knew,' said the young rabbit mournfully. 'All I know is, I feel most peculiar.'

'Like a tummy ache after eating a lot of lettuces, I expect,' she sympathised.

'Worse than that,' said Startup with feeling. 'It's like...' he searched for the right word to express his strange yearnings. But exactly what he thought it was remained a mystery, for at that moment a transformed Fred re-appeared at the top of the steps holding up something in his hand, and yelling triumphantly at the top of his voice. 'Wait till I tell Greta!'

He kissed the notes and tucked them carefully into his top pocket. Then he rode off gaily, scattering letters left and right with wild abandon. 'I'm rich, I'm rich!' His voice wafted back, 'Wot a time we'll have tonight.'

Prudence giggled. 'What a funny man.'

Something caught her attention, and she put her head on one side, listening to the sounds of voices and laughter rising above them.

'What is going on up there, I wonder?' She nudged Startup. 'Come on,' she whispered, 'let's find out.'

As Prudence stole up the steps, Startup found himself following. Watch it, he told himself, this is getting into a habit. Then he realised how silly he was behaving and trotted after her. Shows you what a state you're getting in, he chided himself.

With a final hop, they reached the gate where an extraordinary sight met their gaze.

George was dancing round the lawn, arm in arm with his wife, Joan, waving a bottle of champagne in the air and trying every now and then to pour some of it into a glass his wife was holding.

'Oops,' he was shouting, 'another toast - let's have another toast!'

'What about - Here's to our baby, darling?' reminded his wife.

The mention of baby sent George off into another joyful jig, twirling his wife around till she protested laughing, 'That's enough.'

Immediately, George all concerned rushed away and fetched a deckchair. Prudence and Startup watched open mouthed as he made her sit down, and knelt beside her, holding her hand tenderly.

'Darling Joan,' he said anxiously, 'I can't believe it - our own baby.'

'Isn't it wonderful,' she whispered, 'our very own.'

'What's the matter with them?' whispered Prudence wonderingly. 'Is she ill?'

'They're going to have a baby,' grunted old Ben, appearing briefly out of the long grass.

'But why are they dancing around like that?' said Prudence puzzled.

'That's what humans do when they're in love,' snapped Ben sourly.

At these words, Startup seemed to come out of his dream world, and sprang into the air with a touch of dazed delight.

'That's what's the matter with me,' he cried. 'It's not my tummy-I'm in love!'

'Oh, no,' sighed Prudence, 'not Lola again.'

'I must find her,' said Startup, all of a quiver. 'Don't follow me.'

'I wouldn't think of it,' called Prudence after him. But he was gone.

'Dear Startup, what are we going to do about you?' Prudence shook her head. 'I do hope Grumps has the answer.'

If anyone thought he had the right answer, it was certainly George — although the problems of Startup were furthest from his mind at that moment. For the news about the baby presented a perfect excuse to have an evening out with the lads.

He coughed. 'As you know, dearest, much as I detest these drinking parties at the office, it will be absolutely impossible for me to get away at the usual time, once the news gets around. You know how it is…'

'Yes, George,' his wife agreed placidly.

'Absolutely impossible,' George ploughed on, expecting opposition.

'I said, yes George,' Joan repeated smiling.

'Eh, what was that?' asked George, caught off-guard. Covering his confusion, he felt in his pocket to see how much cash he had to see him through. To his astonishment, he found an empty pocket. 'Dash it, I could have sworn...' he felt around his pockets again, '... I had at least a tenner...'

'Where did you have it last?' asked Joan practically.

'Why, when I was telling Fred about the baby,' said George absently. Then he covered his mouth. 'I must have given it to him.'

'Oh, George, how could you make a mistake like that?'

'Awkward,' decided George after a while, 'distinctly awkward. I say darling, I suppose you couldn't...?'

His wife shook her head sympathetically, and he found himself shaking his in confirmation.

'Sorry, darling, you see...' she started giggling, 'I gave mine to the milkman.'

George half grinned and shrugged his shoulders philosophically. ' Ah, well, I shan't be home so late after all...' But that was where he was wrong, and Startup would have good cause to thank him for it.

Not that Startup wanted to be saved from anything that morning. Now that he had discovered what was the matter with him, he felt like a shipwrecked sailor casting himself adrift in search of land. Only in his case, it was love he was seeking.

It was a strange and exhilarating sensation, just thinking about her. One minute he was up in the clouds, the next minute he was cast down in a trough of despair. He started off memorising all the things she had said to him, and then spent his time analysing the meaning behind every word.

First he remembered all the good things. The way she had looked only at him when they first met. How she seemed interested only in him, and no one else. How she had singled him out to talk to, and had led him away where they could be by themselves...

He smiled blissfully, and shut his eyes letting the memories flood back. Soon he was dancing cheek to cheek with her in his imagination, gliding up and down, and every now and then leaping into the air with a kick of his heels. In other words, he was behaving like Leonard, the Hare. If anything, madder than Hare.

The birds lined up in the trees, cheering him on excitedly, thinking it was great entertainment, and for an encore he pirouetted along the path, holding a flower between his teeth.

Then 'bang', he came out of his dream with a jolt. If she had been so interested in him, why hadn't he seen a sign of her for the past three days? Could it be that she had lost interest in him?

Suddenly the explanation hit him. She had found him dull and stupid after her friends the brown rats. What was it that Puggles had said? 'Don't repeat yourself, Startup. You sound like an idiot.' Now he remembered, he had done nothing else. It was too awful for words. No wonder Prudence had come looking for him when she did. She was trying to stop him making an ass of himself.

'Fool!' he cried fiercely. It was so sudden that Charlie Chaffinch, who was trying to recover from feeding his brood, nearly fell off his perch.

'Fool, yourself,' Charlie called down indignantly.

'Oh, hallo, Charlie,' said Startup embarrassed. 'I didn't mean you, I was talking to myself.' As an explanation, he launched into the saga of his woes, stopping only to blame himself for his stupidity.

Intrigued, Charlie propped open an eye and listened. He had always known the young rabbit to be carefree and completely uninterested in girls, and this sounded serious.

After a while however, Startup got himself so mixed up that the Chaffinch became bored and retired to a higher branch, and sang a plaintive song about the fickleness of women.

When he realised he had lost his audience, Startup paused and tried to make out what the Chaffinch was singing. But it was in rhyming slang and he gave up, banging his head in frustration.

Charlie regarded him calmly. 'Chic-chic. Tree only give you one headache - girl friend give you one long headache, believe you me.'

'You don't know, Lola like I do,' said Startup forlornly.

The chaffinch whistled. 'You don't know her at all, old china. You've only met her once, and she says a few daft things and ping, your imagination does the rest. You're hooked, chum.'

Startup looked perplexed. 'What shall I do, Charlie?'

'Go and find her,' was the instant advice, 'and discover what she's really like.' The chaffinch hopped closer and confided, 'and don't be in such a hurry, or you'll end up like me.' He looked around furtively, 'You'll never believe this, but I only came from the Walter Mitty for a bit of fresh air one weekend, and now see what's happened to me. I'm just a perishing nursemaid.'

With a weary hop, he picked up a biscuit crumb and flew a few yards away where a row of hungry squawking beaks awaited.

Startup sat there for a while digesting his friend's words, then taking fresh heart he started off again looking in a different direction. This time he made for the five acre field where he had last seen Lola. After wandering around in circles he caught sight of a familiar shape outlined against the trees, overlooking the lane.

He gave a whoop of delight and bounded forward. 'Lola!' he called out. 'It's me, Startup.' Shading his eyes against the sun, he thought he saw a flicker of movement nearby, and for a brief moment he imagined there was another shadow next to Lola. He rubbed his eyes, but it was gone.

'Lola?' he said, a little uncertainly.

'Oh, Startup,' Lola stepped forward looking startled. 'Where did you spring from?'

'I was looking for you.' He looked past her. 'Was I interrupting something? I thought I saw someone...'

Lola took one look at his trusting face. 'How sweet,' she trilled breathlessly. 'There's nobody here. I was just whiling the time away thinking of a poem...' she thought quickly, '... about the first time we met. And then you turned up to make it all perfect – how romantic.'

Any suspicions he may have had were immediately blown away like thistledown.

'You were?' he said happily, feeling at the same time he had heard all this somewhere before.

'Yes,' she said firmly in a loud voice, to drown the snigger that was coming from behind the bush.

Something clicked in Startup's mind, but before he could give it a second thought, Lola took hold of his paw and steered him purposefully across the field.

'Let me see,' she prattled on. 'Where shall we go today? I know,' as if the thought had just occurred to her, 'let's take a boat on the river.'

Startup considered the idea and nodded in agreement. Perhaps the peace and tranquillity of the flowing river might give him a chance to get to know her.

'Sounds great.'

Lola gave a slow secretive smile. It was all working to plan, just as Captain Mayfair said it would.

To Startup, the rest of the afternoon had a dreamlike quality. Lola said all the nice things he secretly longed to hear, and not only that, she virtually took command of the outing. All he had to do was to go through the motions of acting as escort, in a drama that might have been rehearsed by others, it was so well arranged.

Lola led the way with a bouncy walk that riveted his attention, and threw extra loving glances over her shoulder. It also had the effect of preventing him from noticing anything going on around them - which was just as well. It seemed only a matter of minutes before they were at the water's edge, although the sun was already sinking towards the horizon.

'Oh, what a lucky thing - there's a boat,' said Lola casually, as if boats had a habit of appearing on the river bank. The sound of their voices made one of the reeds jump, and the rope holding the boat seemed to slip away, as if someone had let go.

'I say, the boat's moving,' observed Startup brightly.

'Oh no, it isn't,' hissed Lola sweetly, her smile slipping a fraction. She nodded her head slightly, and two or three reeds bent towards the rope as it passed, and stopped it. To Startup's amazement, the boat slowly edged its way backwards towards the bank.

'Would you like to get in?' asked Lola absently. Then she answered, as if she was taking both parts of the script. 'Why thank you, dear Startup, I'd love to.' And she stepped in daintily.

Startup was too surprised to think of helping her in, and noticed to his further astonishment that the boat did not rock an inch, even when he gingerly followed her example.

'No, don't sit that end,' said Lola hurriedly, as Startup settled back. 'It's more comfortable over here next to me.'

'But,' protested Startup rather anxiously, 'how can I row from that end?'

'Oh, it's not one of those old fashioned rowing boats,' said Lola gaily. 'We don't need these,' and she deftly slid the oars over the side, producing a muffled howl out of sight.

Startup gulped. 'Are you sure?'

Lola patted the cushion by her side. 'Now come along, otherwise I shall think you don't like me anymore.'

Startup did as he was told, but kept casting glances at the boat to try and work out how it was able to move without any effort, against the flow of the river.

'Tell me,' invited Lola, fluttering her eyebrows invitingly, 'what are you thinking about... now we're alone at last?'

Still mesmerised by the extraordinary behaviour of the boat, Startup said without thinking, 'How do you do it?'

'Anything is easy when you set your heart on it,' purred his companion. 'Tell me,' she murmured, 'have you ever thought how easy it is to fall overboard?'

His mind elsewhere, Startup asked earnestly, 'How do you manage it – without any oars?'

At that moment, a fierce rat clambered over the side of the boat, clasping a huge rock.

'Don't worry about the mechanics of the thing, darling,' said Lola quickly, pulling Startup towards her. 'Just let it happen.' Remembering Charlie's advice, Startup felt he was getting to know Lola too quickly. He tugged himself free, gently at first, and then with all the strength he could muster. When he did manage to break away, he flew back with such speed he butted the rat in the tummy just as the rock was poised ready for delivery. The rat doubled up and dropped the rock straight through the bottom of the boat.

Without saying a word, Lola pointed to the hole and the rat obediently jumped in and wedged himself fast, so that only a trickle of water seeped out.

'You were saying?' remarked Lola, as if nothing had happened.

Startup moved nervously to one side and tried to look over the top of the petrified rat. 'Lola, we've only known each other for a very short time, but I feel you do like me a little, don't you?'

'Oh yes, I do,' assured Lola, nodding her head again. Emboldened by her words, Startup went down on his knees.

At that point, several things happened at one. A noosed rope dropped around the rat's head and shoulders instead, and nearly jerked him out of the hole, letting a lot more water into the boat. Then a spear whistled past Startup's head and pinned Lola to her seat.

When he straightened up to propose, he saw Lola nonchalantly tearing her cloak free.

'Lola,' tried Startup tentatively. 'Could you bring yourself to think of...?'

'Yes, I could,' snarled Lola, losing her temper at the way things were going. 'Kill him!'

At her bidding, a hail of rocks, spears and ropes whistled past their heads. In the middle of the proposal, a sack fell over his head as he tottered towards her side, murmuring, 'Will you marry me?'

By now, dusk was beginning to close in, making it a little difficult for George as he zigzagged up the lane trying to see his way home. An office friend had fortunately dropped him at the bottom of the lane, since he was in no condition to drive, after the generous round of drinks that had been pressed on him.

'That's a rummy kettle of fish,' he managed as he gazed owlishly across the river. He shook his head in disbelief. 'Not possible – absolutely not possible...'

For there in front of him, a rowing boat was careering upstream under its own steam, while a ranting rabbit was shouting at the top of her voice, ordering someone to throw the sack into the water. And the sack itself was hopping about with nobody near it...

In a blind panic, he fell on his face, and yelled at the top of his voice, 'I promise I won't touch another drop - go away, leave me alone!'

He groaned and raised his head again, hoping the ghastly vision would vanish. However, the sound of his voice achieved a far more dramatic effect. The boat immediately veered around and came straight for the bank, with the result that Startup simply shuffled off the side at the moment of impact. Immediately, the boat rose clear of the water, and dozens of rats ran off down the lane, holding it over their heads, with Lola running behind, screaming her head off.

George shuddered and peered through his fingers. Just then, a muddy face appeared through a hole in the sack and inquired hopefully, 'Lola, will you marry me?'

Sometime later when George eventually found his way home, he tried to explain to his wife what he had seen.

Taking one look at him, she merely said, 'Poor George,' and with great understanding led him to the sofa and covered him with a rug.

'You don't understand,' he protested, but the more he attempted to explain it all, the more difficult it became.

As he struggled to find the words, she bent over him and said soothingly, 'How interesting, darling. You must take me to see it tomorrow.'

Seeing her face swimming over him, he finally gave up muttering, 'Absolutely not, old thing...' and passed out.

Chapter Six

Going to the races

'That rabbit is a hopeless case,' said Grumps heavily, at the sight of Startup ambling past at the foot of the tree with his usual dazed look. 'I was counting on him – and now look at him.'

'Completely infatuated, poor lad,' agreed Puggles. Then out of loyalty to his friend, 'Mind you, that Lola woman is enough to turn anyone's head.'

'She's nothing but a spy,' snorted old Owl. 'Anyone can see that.'

'Perhaps he doesn't want to,' said Puggles, getting closer to the truth. Then he added to himself, 'I'm not sure I would, if I were in his shoes.'

But Grumps did not hear, he was sunk in the deepest gloom.

'Our only hope against the brown rats – and what does he do all day?' He banged the nearest window ledge with his beak to give vent to his feelings.

'We must find a way to get through to him – but how?'

Not too far away, someone else was trying to do the same thing, only in a particularly cunning and devious way.

Percy the snake was his name, but he was called all sorts of other, less flattering nicknames such as - 'Sinful Snake' or 'Percy the Sloth' or just plain, 'Percy Artful'. More to the point, he was a very old friend of Captain Mayfair and his rascally band.

'Why hallo, Startup,' he hissed invitingly, slithering forward with deadly charm. 'What's your problem?'

'Problem?' said Startup vaguely. 'Why should I have a problem? I'm in love.'

'Nonsense,' replied Percy complacently. 'Everyone I know has a problem - especially those who think they're in love. What's yours?'

'But I am in love,' insisted Startup, stung out of his reverie. He hesitated and glanced at Percy, half afraid the snake might make fun of him. But Percy gave him a sweet smile he reserved for such occasions.

Reassured, Startup cleared his throat. '... and she cares for me... at least...' he paused and blurted out, 'have you ever heard of a woman acting a bit peculiar... when they say they like you?'

The snake slid a comforting tail around Startup's shoulders. 'All the time, old friend, all the time.'

Rabbit looked at him doubtfully. 'Even when they invite you on their boat, and get their friends to throw things at you...?'

The snake drawled, 'Oh, frequently.'

Startup persevered. 'Like rocks and spears?'

Percy gave a wriggle. 'It happens...'

'And when she says...' Startup faltered, '... kill him – at least, I think she said that – and they threw a sack over me, and tried to tip me in the river?'

'Ugh,' the snake unwound itself with a shudder, and then quickly coiled up again. 'That's what they call a love-hate relationship,' he said hollowly.

'Is it?' said Startup hopefully.

'Why, of course,' snake recovered his poise. 'Everyone knows that.'

'They do?' replied Startup impressed.

''That's just their way of saying, I love you,' enthused Percy, adding casually, 'Have an apple.'

'Why thanks.' Startup took it, not wishing to offend his new found friend. 'I'll have it later.'

'Take a bite now,' urged Percy, hurriedly covering a hole in the apple where he had slipped a pill. 'You'll be surprised what happens when you eat one of these. It's a new type, called forbidden fruit.'

'Oh,' said Startup doubtfully. He took a tentative bite, and immediately felt a most peculiar sensation stealing over him. It began to make him feel sort of confident again, and almost...quite daring. He puffed his chest out. 'I think I see what you mean.'

'That's my boy,' chortled Percy. 'I know a fast operator when I see one. Go get her, boy.'

Startup straightened up. 'All right, I will.' And with an unexpected feeling of elation, he set off with a bouncy swing, with Percy's parting words, 'Let me know how you get on,' ringing in his ears.

His behaviour was not lost on the shrewd old Owl however. Calling Puggles over to the window he pointed testily at the departing figure of Rabbit, making his way purposely across the field. 'Where's he off to now, that's what I'd like to know. He looks as if he's heading for trouble again. Help me down the steps, Puggles old friend. We must get after him, before it's too late.'

Puggles thought quickly. He knew such an exertion would probably be enough to finish his old friend off in his present state of health.

'I tell you what, Grumps,' he said quickly. 'Why don't you stay here and brief Prudence when she comes, while I do the routine shadowing stuff. We don't want the General out on the front line, with only the messenger boy in charge of HQ, do we?'

Grumps halted suspiciously. 'You think I'm too old for it, don't you, I know.' He waved away Puggles protests and gazed anxiously out of the window after Startup, who by now was nearly lost to view.

'I dare say you're right - I'll never catch him now, anyway. Right, of you go. But don't let him out of your sight.'

Puggles heaved a sigh of relief. 'Depend on me.' As he heard Puggles trundling down the stairs, Grumps added half to himself. 'I'll never forgive myself if anything happened to him.'

Although Puggles started off optimistically, he was already beginning to puff a little as he reached the bottom of the tree.

'Oh, foolish Puggles,' he rebuked himself. 'Why don't you wait for Prudence? Never mind, serve you right for volunteering. Well, here goes...' He steeled himself, and marched off with as much dignity as he could muster. To his humiliation, he had only gone a dozen or so paces when he heard Hedgie pipe up next to him, asking if he could join him in a stroll.

'No,' said Puggles shortly. 'I'm in a hurry.'

'Well, slow down a little and you'll have more time,' was the logical answer.

By the time Puggles managed to get away without upsetting his friend and slogged it to the top of the field, Startup was no longer in sight.

'Oh dear,' said Puggles, sitting down and fanning his face with a cabbage leaf. 'Where do we go from here, old lad?'

That was exactly the same thought that was passing through Startup's mind, as he looked across the empty field stretching up to the trees on the skyline. He had been to all the usual places where he would expect to find Lola, without any luck. Where could she be?

While he was puzzling over the next step, he thought he heard a steady drumming noise just the other side of the copse in front of him.

Startup set off to investigate.

When he approached the fringe of the trees, he made his way through them rather cautiously, and then peered out between the branches before venturing into the open again.

To his astonishment, he saw Lola addressing a huge band of rats, stretched out in lines like soldiers on parade. Behind her ran a very deep ditch that seemed to cut the field into two.

At that moment, she raised a paw and at her signal the rats charged towards her. As each line wheeled away in front of her, they hurled their spears at her feet.

By now, the strange and powerful emotions that Percy had inspired seemed to be wearing off. As if to emphasise the fact, the glint of sunlight on the spears made him feel apprehensive. While he was wondering what to do, he came across another apple that Percy had thoughtfully tucked away inside his lunch bag.

He munched away and soon forgot his troubles and any nervousness he may have felt just melted away. Soon, he was on top of the world again, watching the spectacle in mounting wonder, as it was repeated again and again. As soon as he finished, he got up and cleaned his whiskers, then strolled across without a care in the world.

The rats were making so much noise practising that nobody noticed him approaching. In fact, he had to raise his voice several times to make himself heard above the din.

When Lola caught sight of him a sickly smile spread over her face, and she nearly fell into the ditch.

'Why, look who's here!' she called out loudly, trying to attract the attention of the brown rats milling around. 'I said, look who's here!' she repeated, going crimson.

But the brown rats were so intent on perfecting their attack they took no notice, and soon Lola forgot her ladylike image and began screaming at the top of her voice.

Still in his half drugged state, Startup joined in helpfully, adding to the confusion.

By now, Lola was quite beyond herself with rage. She was so frustrated, she snatched a spear from the nearest rat and advanced on Startup herself.

'What a good idea,' beamed Startup. Before she could realise what he was doing, he took the spear out of her hand and stuck it in the ground in front of the next group of rats as they hurtled past.

'That'll make them sit up,' he said satisfied.

The result was absolute chaos. Within seconds, the first row of brown rats went down, the next row tripped over them, and unable to stop, hundreds of others following closely behind shot over their heads into the trench like a pack of cards.

'How's that?' asked Startup, feeling rather pleased with himself.

Lola was beside herself with fury. But to Startup, it only made her look more beautiful.

'You... you...!' she spluttered.

'No, no, you don't have to thank me,' Startup held up a hand modestly.

'Thank you? I'd like to kill you!' she hissed, quite forgetting herself.

'Ah, now that's not strictly true,' corrected Startup confidently.

'Not...what?' she bellowed, taken aback, and the brown rats who had been creeping up on him, watched in fascination.

'No, you see,' announced Startup grandly, 'according to my friend, Percy the Snake, it's all part of the love-hate relationship. It's nothing you need worry about. In fact, I'll be happy to explain it all later when we're alone,' he winked at the rats light-heartedly.

My goodness, you handled that well, he told himself. Already he could see Lola heaving with passion. You can tell she's mad about me, he observed complacently. It's the way she quivers and goes red in the face.

Lola was about to give the order to seize him, when she held back suspiciously. Supposing he's got an army waiting in the woods? He's so sure of himself. Then she thought for a moment. If we can overpower without him being aware of it, we've got him cold and nobody would dare attack.

Mastering her emotion, she smiled cunningly. 'You may be right, Rabbit. What would a silly girl like me know about such things?'

Startup coughed in agreement, and one of the rats sniggered. Lola glared at the offender, and the front row melted back nervously. 'However, while we are delighted to have you here...' she paused to get his reaction, but Startup was following her words with rapt attention. '... perhaps you wouldn't mind helping us out?'

The brown rats immediately looked as if they needed his help, following a steely glance from Lola.

'You see, they are so dangerously keen to win this spear throwing contest. The only trouble is we need someone to pick the winner, and he need to stand right in front of them to judge it all. Not just any old judge, it has to be someone they can respect - a born leader...'

Startup looked suitably coy.

'...someone who's not afraid to stand by his decision...Why,' she looked at him with dawning wonder. 'Of course, it would have to be someone just like you, dear Startup.'

He kicked a tuft of grass nonchalantly. 'I've judged a few tiddlywinks in my time.'

'Then we don't need to look any further,' said Lola softly, looking up at the sky as if her prayers were answered. 'If you're quite certain, dear Startup,' She took hold of him before he could change his mind, and led him to a large stage driven in the ground.

'Why how handy,' she appeared suitably surprised, 'someone's left an old post here - just what we need. Now all you have to do is to stand here, and just to make sure you don't move and put them off while they're aiming, we'll place a few loops around you, like this...'

And in a few seconds, Startup found himself securely trussed to the stake, facing a long line of rats who were licking their lips and testing the edge of their spears.

Feeling a bit exposed, he was beginning to get the feeling that the brown rats no longer looked quite as friendly as he had been led to believe.

Seeing the doubt creeping in, Lola awarded him a winning smile. 'Don't move, Startup dear, otherwise we won't know who the winner is.'

Try as he might, Startup felt there was something wrong with her explanation, but he couldn't quite put his finger on it.

'Find out?' he said with a puzzled laugh. 'I thought I was supposed to pick the winner.' He blinked, 'there must be a simple answer, but I can't quite think what it could be.'

'Oh, but there is, my sweet,' Lola assured him. 'It's the one who gets the closest. And you'll be in the best position to judge. Now just lean back and find out...'

'Like this?' he asked innocently. As he leant back, he noticed the rats raising their spears. 'Why are they looking at me?'

'Shut your eyes and don't worry.' Then she couldn't help adding maliciously, 'It's that love-hate relationship you were talking about, I shouldn't wonder.'

Opening his mouth for a feeble laugh, Startup found his breath cut off in mid-flight by a ring of steel biting into the stake above his head, each shaft still quivering from the force of the throw.

He gulped. 'Is that all there is too it? Why, that's a silly old game. Let's play something else.'

'Wait a minute,' purred Lola in her silkiest tones. 'Now comes the difficult part of the judging. This is where we finish you...I mean, finish it off, if you'll pardon the expression.'

A row of spears appeared from nowhere, all directed at Startup. 'All you have to do is to tell them who the lucky winner is,' she encouraged. 'But I'm glad I'm not in your shoes because there's going to be an awful lot of rotten losers. But, of course, that's why we chose you to do the judging - because we knew you'd be so fearless.'

Startup looked around the row of fierce expressions again and decided he didn't like the idea of being fearless after all.

'Wait,' said Lola, struck by a sudden thought, ''I have a better idea.'

'You have?' he managed hopefully.

'Yes,' smiled Lola. 'I'll have a go - I bet I get closer than anyone.'

She slowly selected a spear and ran her finger over the tip while Startup watched hypnotised.

'Any last requests?'

'Have you an apple?' was all Startup could think of, remembering wistfully how different he felt when he had one earlier.

'A what?' repeated Lola, put off her stroke.

'An apple,' said Startup faintly above the sniggers and other rude ratty comments.

'What a splendid idea,' cried Lola. 'I can split it on your head - such courage.' She shook her head in reluctant admiration, and eyed the rats. 'What do you think?'

The rats looked at each other uneasily.

'A pear or an orange then. Come, we must be fair.'

Srtartup began to perk up. 'No, it must be an apple,' he said firmly.

'Well?' glared Lola, then tired of waiting, she yanked a black helmet off one of the rats who yelped.

'Serve you right for tightening the straps,' she snapped. 'Right, this will do.'

She placed the helmet on Startup's head where it rested lopsided over one ear, and he realised with sinking heart that his ruse had failed.

'Stand back, everyone,' she commanded. 'Ready, Rabbit?'

Startup flung a last desperate look around, but there was no sign of anyone coming to his rescue. Just then the helmet fell forward over his face, and cut off whatever he was going to say. Which was just as well, for if he had been able to see what was coming next he would have fainted clean away.

Lola balanced the spear with surprising ease and raised it back ready to throw. 'Now then,' she cried. 'See if I can pot the black.'

Just as she released the spear, an extraordinary event happened. The ground at the edge of the trench started to crumble and began caving in, and some of the rats disappeared into it. The stake slowly turned sideways, and the spear only struck a glancing blow before the whole stake toppled over.

Everyone froze, rooted to the spot. Then in front of their mesmerised gaze, some of the rats who were still sprawled in the trench seemed to rise up on the back of a hideous black shape emerging from the depths.

'Aaaaah!' The brown rats huddled together gibbering with fear, then turned as one, falling over each other in a desperate attempt to get away from the monstrous form advancing on them. Even Lola blanched with fear, and fled with the rest of them, rapidly overtaking them in a blind rush.

Had they waited, they would have found out that the monster could talk as well. With a sigh of satisfaction, he wiped a thick clump of mud off his face and murmured, 'Now that's what I call a mud bath.' Then remembering what he was there for, Puggles ambled over to the trench and started chewing at the ropes holding Startup to what was left of the stake.

As the bonds fell away, Startup grinned shakily at his friend. 'Thanks, Puggles, how did you get here?'

'It was nothing, dear boy,' replied Puggles modestly. 'I just happened to be passing, and caught sight of Lola and her thugs, and realised they were up to no good.'

What he didn't explain was how he had crawled for what seemed hours along the bottom of the trench to reach his friend without being seen, so that he could loosen the earth around the foot of the stake. 'Anyway, I'm glad I got here in time- my word, you had a narrow shave there, old lad.'

To his friend's bewilderment, Startup dusted himself down and remarked airily. 'Oh, I assure you I was in no danger. Lola's friends are perfectly harmless. They were only playing.' He puffed out his chest. 'They asked me to judge their spear competition.'

'Nonsense,' said Puggles shortly. 'You were being lined up as the number one target when I arrived.'

'Me?' said Startup with maddening cheek. 'Lola wouldn't do a thing like that to me - why, we're getting married you know. I was perfectly safe.'

'Well, in that case, you don't need me anymore,' growled Puggles, getting very cross. 'I'm going to have a proper clean-up this time, to get rid of the nasty smell of those brown rats. Good day to you.'

And he mumbled to himself as he walked away. 'That'll teach you to try and help your old friends, Puggles my boy. They don't deserve it.'

'Wait!' called out Startup hastily. 'You don't understand.' Then his defences dropped and he cried out, 'I can't help it...'

But it was too late. Puggles had already lumbered straight into the ditch with an almighty splosh that drowned out his words.

Startup stood there undecided for a moment, then gave a great sigh and turned for home.

Chapter Seven

Riding high

Next day, the weather was perfect. Although the long hot summer days were drawing to a close, everyone agreed over breakfast that it was going to be just right. Hardly a wisp of cloud disturbed the deep blue sky, and the air was as crisp as a spring lettuce. For this was the day all the animals had been waiting for - Hookwood's Grand Summer Fete.

Since it was started many years ago (nobody could remember exactly when or why - even old Grumps had to scratch his head about it), the fete had become the most popular happening in the animals' calendars.

All thoughts of any threats from the brown rats, real or imaginary, were quickly swept away as preparations for the event got under way. From early light, there was an air of bubbling expectancy, all centred on the five acre field where the Fete was always held. Trestle tables were being set up in different parts of the field, and tents were mushrooming in all shapes and sizes.

Old feuds were quickly forgotten as each of the animals made his or her special contribution. Dora was busy laying out a table full of delicious vegetable pies, and directing Ben where to put the tomato and cucumber drinks.

Clara Goose was unpacking some woollens she had specially knitted for the occasion (they were all her size, so she was hoping to get them all back again), while Leonard held the box for her. He felt very foolish doing so, but pretended he was addressing a meeting and wore his distant vague smile.

Oswald the Duck was guarding the 'guess the weight competition' cake, and was helpfully trimming the edges with his beak - *just* to make it look more presentable, he explained, but nobody believed him.

Even Tug the Robin was doing his bit, searching for worms that he said he was going to sell for bait. But he didn't have a bucket to put them in, so nobody believed him either. Nearby, Spike the worm wasn't taking any chances, and kept well away.

Out of the seeming chaos of flags and bunting going up, and stalls being filled to overflowing, and animals swarming in all directions, the figure of Squire Nabbit could be seen striding importantly to and fro, inspecting everything as if it was his sole responsibility. Fortunately, nobody took the slightest notice, with the result that he looked a trifle foolish.

From his vantage point, Grumps the Owl was keeping a watchful eye on what was going on, and muttering to himself that he could have done it all a darn sight better. But he was thoroughly enjoying himself all the same.

While high above them all, from an upstairs window in Oak Tree Cottage, George's wife took one look at the bustling activity and hurriedly pulled the blind down in the hope that her husband, George wouldn't notice.

If she had glanced up at the sky she would have seen an extraordinary sight. A gaily coloured balloon was slowly swinging into view over the trees and from a basket suspended underneath some figures were leaning out and waving handkerchiefs. Normally, such an unusual occurrence would have drawn crowds from miles around, but today it was treated as just another attraction, part of the Grand Fete atmosphere.

Soon the balloon was safely tethered in the corner of the field, and as there were still a lot of jobs to be done to get the Fete ready in time, the animals went back to work without sparing it a second glance. Had they done so, they might have thought it curious that none of the passengers appeared to be getting out. Grumps idly swung his telescope over and inspected the balloon and its occupants. One small point bothered him slightly, but a new group of visitors started flying in and he quickly forgot about it.

This year, the news had obviously been passed from wing to wing, for not only were there all the old familiar faces like Matty the Moorhen from Moorhouse Wood, Rosy Tern from Tipperary and Razor Bill from Portsmouth, but there were also old and new faces from overseas. First to arrive were some Graylag Geese from Iceland, then Brent Geese from Greenland, followed by a pair of Spoonbills from Holland, Pierre Prochard the young bachelor from Paris, the Widgeons from Wyoming, a party of Mandarin Ducks from Peking, and Carl Bunting, a refugee from Berlin.

The sight of all these new arrivals put fresh heart into the toiling workers. Particularly when Hiram and Edna Widgeon landed with an overnight bag stuffed with dollar bills.

To set the seal on the prestigious event, the sun rose above the hills, spreading its friendly presence over Hookwood and bringing a smile to all the animals' faces.

All, that is, except Startup's.

For Startup was in disgrace. When his mother heard how badly he had behaved towards his friend Puggles, she took away his supper just as he was about to start eating. As far as he was concerned, it was worse than being packed off to bed without seeing any food.

Visions of that piled up plate haunted him, and he found himself tossing and turning all night, feeling all mixed-up and sorry for himself. For the hundredth time he couldn't help wondering how on earth he had got into such a mess. On the morning of the Fete he had woken up muttering, 'Why me?' He repeated the question as he looked at himself in the mirror and added for good measure, 'What have I done?'

It all started when he met Lola. Ever since then everything had changed and for the worse. If this is what love does to you, you can keep it, he thought miserably, and jamming on a beret belonging to his father, he set off in a rebellious mood. After a while, his better nature came to his rescue, and he told himself guiltily that he must call on his old friends and apologise.

So he made his way to the sty at the bottom of the garden and knocked on the battered old door. There was nothing to be heard except for some heavy breathing the other side. He knocked again and suddenly there floated through a crack in the door the unmistakable sound of Puggles snoring in a snorty ruffled sort of way.

'Come on, Puggles, I know you're there,' he called out. Just then a plank was thrust through a hole and Startup read the scrawled message, 'We are not at home,' and underneath, 'specially to ungrateful rabbits'.

'Puggles, listen!' shouted Startup, 'I've come to say I'm sorry.' But all he could hear were loud and repeated snoring noises. Giving up, he kicked at the plank and turned away, feeling fed up and unsure what to do. After lolloping around without any idea where to go, he drifted towards five acre field and sat down listlessly to watch the preparations - in a half-hearted manner. And this is where Prudence found him.

'Oh hallo, Startup,' she said simply, not wanting him to know she had been looking for him for hours. 'I didn't see you there. Can I join you?'

'Why not?' he sighed, 'Nobody else wants to.'

'Have you seen, Puggles?' asked Prudence after a while. 'Grumps wants to have a word with him.'

'I hope he has better luck than I did,' said Startup with feeling. 'He won't speak to me.'

'Why, what's wrong?' asked Prudence tactfully, having already heard the facts from Puggles at great length.

Startup sighed again. He couldn't bring himself to admit to Prudence of all his friends how wrong he had been about Lola. After a great many promptings and hesitation, he began to describe his latest encounter, and found himself exaggerating his own role to such an extent it sounded as if he had been defending Lola single-handed against a horde of brown rats.

'Didn't Puggles have something to do with it, as well?' asked Prudence, going a little pink.

'Oh, he did give me some help.' admitted Startup. But he was well into the swing of it by now, and began to feel a little indignant about the way his word was being doubted.

'Actually, he thought I was being captured, and when I tried to explain, he got it all wrong. And now he's gone into a sulk, and refuses to see me.'

Prudence took a deep breath and counted up to ten. 'I really think you ought to hear his side of it, Startup,' she said at last. 'After all, he is one of your oldest friends.'

Rabbit wriggled uncomfortably. 'I tried, what more do you want?'

'Go and see him,' urged Prudence. 'I'm sure he didn't mean it. I'll come with you, if you like.'

'No,' said Startup, feeling more mixed up than ever. 'Later, I'll see him later. Promise.'

And with that he excused himself, and made his way quickly to the Fete to lose himself in the friendly isolation of the crowd.

On the way, he almost ran into an elegant butterfly. It was so beautifully dressed, he gaped at the colours. He was even more astonished when the butterfly greeted him like a long lost friend.

'Hail, Startup. How's life treating you?'

Startup blinked. The voice was certainly familiar, but it didn't look a bit like anyone he knew. While he was furiously turning over names and places in his mind, the butterfly came to his rescue.

'You remember? Algernon, the caterpillar?'

Startup peered at him, even more confused. 'Of course, but...'

'Yes, I know, quite stylish, eh?' The butterfly preened itself. 'A bit different from that scruffy little urchin you used to know, I grant you. Anyway, enough of that – what's with you, as they say. You haven't gone all parochial and settled down, have you?'

His man-about-town tone, and the way he said it was all the encouragement Startup needed. He swallowed, and without further ado launched into his escapades featuring the lovely Lola.

His friend whistled. 'That Lola sounds quite a dish – a little strong for some, no doubt. What she wants is someone quite masterful.' And he fluttered his wings again, as if he was absolutely clear in his mind who that someone should be.

'But what can I do?' cried Startup desperately. 'I can't give her up, but I can't live without her.'

Algernon gave him a cool look of appraisal. 'My dear fellow, nothing could be simpler. You've seen what the bee does? He flits from one flower to another, and simply helps himself to any honey he wants on the way. That's exactly my philosophy. Don't get trapped by any old flower that flutters her petals at you - spread your favours like the wise old bee.'

Seeing Startup hesitate, he nudged him. 'It's a short and gay life, old lad. Take my word for it, and make the most of what comes along. Such a change from being a stodgy old caterpillar, you've no idea. Fancy plodding around with all those feet, day after day. Cost me a fortune in shoe leather, believe me.'

He gave a little whirl. 'Now look at me. A fine pair of wings and a nifty turn of speed. What more do you want?' Fluttering his wings dreamily, he gave happy sigh. 'I spend all my days gadding about after the girls. That's what you need – a touch of the flitters. You don't know what you're missing.'

'You think I should?' asked Startup doubtfully.

Algernon tapped him on the shoulder with an air of knowing authority. 'I'm absolutely sure of it.'

Rabbit scratched his head and thought about it. Perhaps if he had more than one girl friend, it wouldn't hurt so much. Then he thought about it some more, and the more he thought about it, the more attractive it began to sound.

'Where do I start?' he asked simply.

His friend gazed pityingly and waved at the Fete. 'Look about you, Startup, my old lad. The whole world is your oyster.'

As if on cue, the loudspeaker made some spluttery noises. Then the announcer was abruptly cut off when Oswald the Duck noticed a number of strange wires leading from the microphone and started chewing them.

Unaware she could no longer be heard, Josie the Giraffe was finding it very difficult to make herself heard over the loudspeaker, unaware that some busybody had moved the microphone down to grown level, thinking that Hedgie, the hedgehog, was going to make the announcements – quite forgetting that he needed at least a day to get there. Suddenly she caught sight of a strange shape in the sky, and forgot all about what she was doing in her efforts to tell everyone about the approaching object that seemed to appear from nowhere over their heads.

But someone had already got the message. Rosy Tern was jumping up and down so much, she nearly overturned the tea urn.

'Will you look at that, me darlings. It's another of them, sure and fancy.'

Just then, a large shadow fell across them, and looking up Startup saw a flapping balloon drifting sideways overhead and a beautiful oriental face peering down at him.

'What are you waiting for?' urged Algernon, with a wide grin. 'I bet it's you she's interested in.'

'Me?' said Startup blankly.

'Yes, don't waste time. Go to it.' Algernon gathered himself. 'Must fly.'

With that he was away, leaving Rabbit feeling strangely alone in the middle of the crowd.

He glanced around undecided, and then caught sight of the attractive girl again as the balloon gently touched down. To his surprise she beckoned him, and without thinking what he might be getting himself into he made his way in her direction.

The sight of yet another balloon tugged at a chord in Owl's mind, making him take a second look at the passengers in the basket.

Whatever it was he saw caused him to reach hurriedly for a mirror he kept for a special emergency. He began flashing it from the sun into the crowds, hoping that Prudence could see it, wherever she was. It was only by the merest chance that Prudence noticed the winking light. The thought of Startup falling out with his old friend Puggles made her feel sad, and for a moment she was lost in memories, recalling all the good times they had had together.

I must keep an eye on Startup, she resolved and see that he doesn't get into any more mischief. She pulled herself up and scanned the faces in the crowd without success. It was at that moment as she turned away that she caught a fleeting glimpse of a dancing light in the tree tops.

At first she ignored it, but then with a rush of apprehension she remembered it was the signal to say Grumps needed her in a hurry.

'Golly,' she started worrying, 'I wonder what's happened now.'

There was a good reason to be worried where Startup was concerned. He was now on the fifth, or was it his sixth hospitality drink. It started when the slant-eyed beauty had asked him to join her in a toast to celebrate their win in the balloon race.

Startup was too polite to ask who they were competing against, particularly as there only seemed to be one other balloon around. But by then he was too mesmerized by her liquid eyes to argue. Even when she introduced him to the Captain he didn't hear any warning bells. He was so relaxed he neither knew nor cared. Glasses kept on being thrust at him, and out of natural bunny courtesy he didn't like to refuse.

'Have another fizzyade,' the fat balloonist beamed, placing a bear-like arm around him.

'Try this one first,' insisted the slant-eyed girl, stirring a drink vigorously.

Startup watched hypnotised. It was just how his mother always mixed his medicine, he thought owlishly. He took an experimental sip. It even tasted like medicine, nasty and bitter.

'I know why you call it a hospitality drink,' he joked. 'One glass and you end up in hospital.'

He looked from one to the other. They both seemed to be waiting for something to happen.

'You look as if you are waiting for something to happen,' he voiced his thoughts.

Their faces swam in and out of focus until Startup experienced a sudden feeling of familiarity.

'You know,' he said at last, concentrating on getting each word out. 'I think I know you.'

He tried to pull himself upright, and for a moment the oriental face stiffened and the Captain fumbled at his pocket.

Startup moved to put the drink down but found he had no strength left. A gleam of triumph flitted across the Captain's face and at that moment Startup knew.

'Why, you're Captain Mayfair!' he accused weakly. He swayed towards the girl who shrank back.

'And you must be…' But before he could get the words out, he pitched forward on his face.

Grumps caught his breath as he surveyed the scene through his telescope. 'Where's Prudence?' he exclaimed fretfully. 'Startup's in dreadful danger.' He whirled anxiously, 'Ah, there you are.'

Before Prudence could utter a word, he thrust the telescope in her hands. 'Tell me what you see, I can't bear it.'

Prudence peered fearfully in the lens. 'There's a man and a woman propping someone up in the balloon.'

Grumps groaned. 'They've drugged him, the fiends.'

'…Drugged who?' Prudence looked up at the old man and paled in sudden understanding. 'You mean…' she took another look and stiffened. 'The girl is kissing the fat man and he's pinning a medal on her.'

'For her part in tricking Rabbit, no doubt,' muttered Grumps feverishly. 'That's Captain Mayfair, the Russian spy, and his fancy girl friend.'

'You don't mean – Lola?' burst out Prudence, and then she noticed something. 'Wait…he's moved. Startup's moved!'

'Here, let me see,' said Owl sharply, and pulled the eyepiece towards him. 'You're right, and they don't seem to have noticed.'

'Oh, what can we do?' implored Prudence. 'We can't just stand here and watch.'

Wise Owl pondered. 'Somehow we have to find a way of distracting their attention. I know,' he cried, bouncing up and down excitedly, 'we've got to capture the other balloon.'

'But...but why, and how are we going to do that?' She asked, beginning to wonder if he had lost his grip, but as he outlined his plans a flicker of hope lit up her face.

Without further ado, Grumps whisked away a rug in the corner, revealing a slumbering shape.

'Hedgie?' exclaimed Prudence. 'How can he help?'

The old owl carefully wrapped up the prickly animal in a towel and handed him over to Prudence. As he did so, he whispered what he wanted her to do in case their friend woke up.

'Now keep still,' said Prudence firmly, heading for the stairs, 'I want it to be a lovely surprise for those nasty brown rats.'

'While you're doing that,' called Grumps after her, 'I'll round up some of our friends at the Fete. But it's up to you, Prudence. Good luck!'

'Thanks,' said Prudence to herself as she pushed through the crowd, making for the second balloon tethered a little farther back. 'I shall need it.' Quaking inwardly, she pulled herself up and peered into the basket, expecting to be challenged any minute.

Luckily, the crew were engrossed in hauling out bags of ballast from the bottom of the basket ready for leaving, and had no idea what was going to happen. Seeing this, Prudence smiled and gleefully unwrapped her precious bundle. With a quick heave, she dropped the now fully awaked Hedgie upside down on the bending row of backs.

Immediately, pandemonium broke out as snarling figures darted to and fro with screams of anguish, emptying the basket in a flash.

'Now,' said Prudence thoughtfully surveying the scene. 'I wonder how this thing works?'

Meanwhile in the other balloon, Startup tried to pretend he was still unconscious, as he listened to his enemies discuss what to do with him. He was particularly outraged at the way Lola was making up to the Captain and realized with heavy heart that he had been completely fooled by her all along.

'I think my dear that we will have to make it look like an accident,' the Captain was saying smoothly, peeling off his disguise. 'So when we get high enough, we must remember to cut his ropes.'

'You mean, he was looking over the side and got dizzy and we couldn't get to him in time,' suggested Lola, catching on.

Captain Mayfair's reply was drowned in a sudden outburst of voices rising indignantly outside.

Matty the Moorhen was squawking; Rosy Tern was singing Irish ballads in a very loud voice; Razor Bill was waving a cutlass and inviting anyone and everyone to take him on, and Pierre Pochard was trying to outdo Rosy Tern with a gay Parisian number. Then a party of Mandarin ducks joined in and Carl Bunting started shouting, 'Down with the tyrants!'

It was getting so noisy that Captain Mayfair recoiled uneasily, and looked even more uncertain when Lola demanded he should do something.

While this was going on, Startup had been desperately twisting his paws out of sight to free himself. Recognizing some of the voices, he felt a surge of hope. While the Captain and Lola were engaged in a heated argument with Grumps' friends, he saw his chance and hobbled to the side of the basket.

'Quick, jump for it, Startup!' came a piercing whisper. He looked up unbelievingly, and there, joy of joys, was Prudence waving at him from another balloon only a few yards away. Scrambling up with some difficulty, he waited until the basket swung his way again and with a quick prayer launched himself across the narrowing gap. There was a sudden shout of rage behind him, but then he was across, falling in a heap on top of some ballast.

'Help me free!' gasped Startup. 'We've got to get rid of the ballast, otherwise we'll never get away.'

'I've got a better idea,' giggled Prudence, and picking up Hedgie, she pressed him against the skin of the balloon and he nearly passed out with the sudden release of gas.

'That'll make us go down, not up,' cried Startup horrified. 'They'll easily catch us now.'

'Good, that's what I want them to think,' laughed Prudence, and coolly cut his ropes.

'Get ready to throw the ballast out when I give the word.'

'That's a smart move,' said Startup with understanding. He was beginning to see new qualities in her that he never before knew existed.

Prudence glanced up. 'Here they come. I see your friend Lola's on board. Is she still up to her old tricks?'

'Yes,' said Startup, relieved at the way she was taking it. 'You were quite right about her,' he admitted honestly. 'Oh, and thanks for the rescue.'

But he didn't need to thank her. The knowledge that he no longer had any interest in the wicked Lola was all she needed, and all at once everything was fine again.

'Look out,' called out Startup. 'We seem to be landing on the brown rats headquarters.'

There was a shriek of triumph above, and looking up Startup saw the Captain dancing up and down, shaking his fist in delight.

Pretending to be frightened, Startup ducked down out of sight and reached for a couple of bags of ballast, ready to heave them overboard at the crucial moment. A few seconds later, he found Prudence at his side holding another one.

'This should take care of a handful of the stinkers at the same time,' said Startup cheerfully.

Prudence eyed the Captain's balloon as it drifted towards them, and whispered something in Startup's ear.

An even bigger grin appeared on his face. 'You betcha,' he agreed happily.

Just as they were dropping to within touching distance of the scurrying rats below who were hugging themselves in anticipation, Prudence leaned across and let go her lethal bomb on the henchman in charge, catching him smartly on the head.

'Bullseye!' cried Startup, leaning over the side.

Then with a swish, the other balloon slid past. Captain Mayfair was hanging out, with one leg stuck in the rope ladder, impatient to be down and capture his prisoners personally.

'Now,' said Prudence coolly, and without warning Startup lobbed his bags of ballast right into the enemy's basket, giving the two surprised passengers an unexpected present in passing.

Loaded down with the extra weight, the Captain's balloon shot straight down, completely enveloping the swarm of brown rats beneath.

Immediately, Prudence's balloon – for there was no doubt who was Captain on this trip – shot up as if by magic and swept away to high ground and safety.

Chapter Eight

The brown rats move in

'Take a seat, old lad,' said Puggles cordially.

It was a week later. All signs of the brown rats and the notorious Captain Mayfair and Lola had vanished virtually overnight, and life at Hookwood was back to normal.

Despite the apparent calm, Startup had the uneasy feeling that they hadn't seen the last of the brown rats, but Puggles poo-pooed it. 'Nonsense, my dear fellow.'

'All the same...' worried Startup, and jumped at the sound of a knock on the door. But it was only their friends, Prudence and Grumps, the wise Owl.

'Leave the door open,' said Prudence. 'Hedgie will be along in a moment.'

'Well, we can't wait that long,' announced Puggles humorously, getting to his feet. 'Now chums, I've asked you here to my sty-lish abode...' he paused for a laugh, but Grumps muttered, 'Get on with it,' and he continued with a pained expression.

'As I was going to say, before you chaps joined us, now that all that awful business is well and truly over and done with, I say - why don't we celebrate?'

He beamed around expansively at everyone. There was a pause, while everyone thought about it.

Then Prudence smiled. 'What a super idea. What does anyone else think about it?'

'Well, I have mentioned it to one or two friends,' said Puggles modestly. 'And they all think it's a good wheeze.'

'They would do,' grunted Owl. 'That's all they think about - feeding and drinking.'

'What do you say, Startup?' asked Prudence, seeing her friend staying rather quiet about it.

'Oh, I don't mind a do,' said Startup slowly, 'It's just...'

'Don't listen to him,' broke in Puggles benevolently, 'He still thinks those brown rats are hanging around, waiting for a chance to have another go at us. I ask you – has anyone seen a single one of those beastly creatures within miles of here in the last few days?'

'No,' said Prudence thoughtfully. 'But I know what Startup means. It does seem strange that they disappeared so quickly.'

Startup looked at her gratefully. 'That's exactly how I feel about it. It just doesn't make sense.'

'Does it matter?' asked Puggles. 'Let's be thankful that they've gone, and don't be afraid to say so. After all, it's not often we get a chance like this. And what a marvellous way to round off the summer. We can have singing and dancing, and dancing and...feasting, and...'

'Did I hear you say feasting?' said a voice hopefully, and there was Hedgie poking his head around the corner of the doorway. 'I do hope you'll have baked leaves and worm pie. Very tasty that.'

Grumps sniffed. 'Trust you to turn up when food's mentioned.'

'Well, I don't care what you all say,' grumbled Puggles defiantly, 'I still think it's a good idea.'

'I didn't say I disagreed,' said Grumps mildly.

'Eh?' Puggles was astonished. 'Does that mean you're in favour?'

'I don't go in for such wasteful occasions usually,' snapped Grumps. 'But there are special moments in all our lives when I consider it right to give thanks, and this is one of them. In answer to your question, Puggles, the answer is an unqualified yes. And close your mouth when you're not speaking - it creates a draught.'

He turned to Startup, as Puggles fell back in amazement.

'I can well see your point, young Rabbit, but we can't spend the rest of our lives worrying about whether they are coming back, or not. But I can tell you what we can do about that...' And the others moved up to hear what he had to say.

'Right, are you all listening? This is what I suggest we do. To make sure we don't get any intruders, we'll post a strong guard and have an extra lookout at the oak tree. As for the party, we'll hold that in the barn at the bottom of the garden. What do you say to that?'

There were nods of approval, and Startup brightened up at the mention of a guard and began to warm to the idea.

Seeing his change of heart, Prudence gave a big sigh of relief. 'Good, when shall we have it then?' She asked in a practical manner.

'I say, as soon as possible,' said Puggles eagerly.

'We need more time,' the wise Owl silenced him with a frown. 'There's all kinds of things to be planned - decisions to be made.'

'Like what shade of mud I should use...' said Puggles gravely.

'You look lovely as you are,' giggled Prudence.

'Dates first,' said Owl sternly. 'What about three weeks this Saturday? That'll be... let me see, the 23rd.'

A voice came unexpectedly from the doorway. 'Make it the 24th.'

'Oh, it's you, Ben,' acknowledged Owl. 'What difference does a day make?'

Old Ben looked around proudly. 'Because it's my boy's birthday, that's what.'

There were cries of surprise and congratulations. 'What a great idea,' said Prudence gladly. 'I'd no idea it was your birthday, Startup.'

'That means we'll have to buy a present,' groaned Hedgie.

'Why, thanks, Hedgie,' grinned Startup. 'Tell you what...I wouldn't mind one of those phew machines, like Fred the postman's got.'

'What's a 'phew' machine?' asked Puggles mystified.

'It's what the postman calls it every time he gets off,' explained Startup.

'I think Hedgie could do with one of those,' guffawed Puggles. 'But what a splendid thought — a double celebration.' There was such a bubble of excitement after that remark that nobody noticed a shadow fall across the doorway.

Outside, Leonard the Hare listened with great interest at what was being planned. Then he stole away, a sly smile creeping over his face.

The day of celebrations had come and gone...well almost gone. Puggles was on his feet — well almost on his feet — making the last toast of the evening.

'Ladies and gentlemen,' he swayed, choosing his words with great care.

'This is the last thank you of the evening. It is for all those sterling friends who have given their time unstinkingly - er, or should I say, gladly for the occasion. Quietly and efficiently, without thought of any thanks or reward...' A note of surprise crept onto his voice. '... In particular, I would like to single out... someone who I must confess I don't usually see offering his services quite so willingly as he has done this evening - Leonard Hare, who has so generously helped prepare the wine - even uncorking it himself.' Puggles led the clapping to a few murmurs of disbelief.

Startup glanced up quickly. At that moment, Hare started backing away, in a particularly furtive manner that immediately aroused his suspicions. A dozen thoughts flashed through his mind as he looked at Prudence for a clue.

'The wine,' she gasped.

On his feet in an instant, Startup shouted a warning. 'Stop, don't touch the drinks...' But as he spoke, the room started to revolve, and his legs felt curiously weak.

'Nonsense,' beamed Puggles. He sipped his wine appreciatively. 'My word, this is good strong stuff.' He looked around. 'Wake up you lot - you don't know what you're missing.'

He was speaking to himself. By now, most of the guests were already nodding off over the table, some in the middle of a sentence.

In the background, Hare finished fumbling with the door and stepped back. The next minute the room was full of brown rats.

Wrapped in his thoughts, Puggles carried on pondering about the quality of the wine, even while he was being lifted off his feet.

'Definitely above average,' he pronounced at last. 'In fact, there's quite a lift to it.' He nodded to the assembled company, 'Anytime you want your wine tested, you can put me down.'

He suddenly looked down in bewilderment at the grinning invaders, as if seeing them for the first time.

'I say, dash it, put me down!'

They obliged immediately by dropping him on the floor with a thump.

As he got up grumbling, an unexpected hush fell on the group. The sea of brown rats fell back and through the middle strode Captain Mayfair and Lola, followed by the fearful sight of the Black Rat himself. Black Freddie, King of the Rats.

Strolling jauntily towards the table, King Freddie smiled evilly at the cowering rats and glanced with contempt at the unconscious figures sprawled across the table.

'So, I've got you at last.' He grinned, showing a row of broken, crooked teeth, and strode up and down in his element.

Prudence watched him come nearer. At last, he stood looking down with satisfaction at the still figure of Startup.

'Especially this one,' he added. 'I've been waiting for this opportunity for a long time.'

'Don't you dare,' spoke up Prudence bravely. 'You wouldn't say that if he were awake.'

Black Freddie looked around slowly, his scowl changing to a smile of wolfish pleasure at the sight of her.

'Why, what a charming rabbit.' And with an extravagant bow, he swept his plumed hat off so low that the feathers brushed the floor.

Prudence suddenly caught sight of Startup stirring and wildly said the first thing that came into her head, to keep him from noticing.

'You won't get away with it. You haven't caught everyone, you know.'

Black Freddie darted a look at her and sneered. 'You seem very confident, my dear. And who do you think we've missed, eh? We've got the whole village here.' He waved an arm at the sleeping guests to emphasise his point.

'There's Wise Owl, for one,' she blurted out, then froze with horror at what she'd said. Please let him get away, she prayed to herself, please!

A smile of unconcealed satisfaction spread over his face. 'Major Podge!' Black Freddie bawled.

A tall angular figure broke ranks and came smartly to attention. ' Sir!'

'Tell the young lady what it was you found at the oak tree.'

Major Podge drew himself up and repeated parrot fashion. 'Acting on information received from Hare, Sir, we sent in an assault party and were set upon by an owl and a duck who we despatched.'

'You mean... Owl is dead?' gulped Prudence, turning pale.

'That's all, Major.' King Freddie hastily dismissed him.

'He wasn't hurt, I promise you, young lady.' He prodded Startup, making him groan. 'See, like your friend, he's just having a little nap - as all the others.'

Prudence saw he was speaking the truth for once. The other guests were already beginning to stir. Some were sitting up, and others staggering to their feet. But they did not get far. Any that tried to push their way through were seized and thrown back to join the rest, amid jeers and laughs from the brown rats.

'You will be my special guest,' promised Black Freddie after a lingering glance. 'But first I must work out our plans for a special...celebration.' His eyes rolled at the prospect. 'Your servant, ma'am.' He gave another bow and sauntered away to speak to Captain Mayfair.

'Startup, are you alright?' fretted Prudence, trying to help him up. All she could hear was a faint groan and when she bent down she was startled to see him open his eyes briefly and wink at her.

'Pretend I'm ill,' he whispered, scarcely moving his lips. She nodded, greatly relieved. Afraid she might give herself away, she just sat there without moving. She needn't have worried. By the sound of the raised voices behind her, it was quite clear that nobody was taking the slightest notice.

'And I say, let's get rid of them now,' she heard Captain Mayfair insist.

'Yes, kill them all,' urged Lola shrilly.

Black Freddie silenced them with a snarl. 'If you'd done everything I told you, we would have caught them long ago, but for your fumbling. So don't try and tell me. I caught them, so I'll deal with them.'

'But supposing they get away again?' wailed Lola.

'They won't get away this time,' growled Black Freddie. 'I have a special treat in store. A duel to the death with the Rabbit, and as for the pretty one...' he laughed. 'I have other plans for her.'

Wheeling around, he pointed to the two rabbits. 'Seize them!'

'Startup, what can we do?' cried Prudence as the mob surged forward.

'We'll think of something,' muttered Startup, without much conviction. He fingered a lucky charm, his birthday present from Prudence. 'We'd better.'

Unaware of the high drama in the barn, another guest was on his way to join the festivities, especially groomed for the event. He had taken so much trouble that he had worn out two old brooms he found up by the cottage to get his prickly overcoat just right.

Fortunately as it turned out, Hedgie never allowed himself enough time to prepare himself for any social gathering. So when the hedgehog finally arrived there was nobody there to ask for his ticket.

'That's odd,' he thought, 'I distinctly remember Owl saying it was the 24th.' Then another thought struck him.

'And not a guard to be seen anywhere - perhaps I got the date wrong after all.'

Just as he was debating whether to face up to the prospect of missing out on his worm pie, he heard a sudden commotion inside.

Suddenly the door was flung open and Prudence burst through. 'Help!' she yelled. 'It's the brown rats! Tell the village…' She gazed wide-eyed past Hedgie, without seeing him. The next minute she was pounced on and dragged back inside.

Hedgie swallowed, 'Oh, gracious. I must get help. Oh my word and Jeremy Spilkin.' Jeremy was the name he always called upon in his hour of need. But now the moment had come, he really couldn't remember where Jeremy was. And the longer he considered the problem, the more confused he got, until after a while he could scarcely remember who Jeremy was.

By then it was getting on, and Hedgie began to panic.

Steady on, he started telling himself, 'don't get your needles in a knot.' He turned vaguely in the direction of the oak tree hoping Owl might still be there. He placed great faith in his friend Owl. Owl would be sure to know what to do, he consoled himself. Or I might even meet someone on the way.

It so happened that the oak tree was quite close to where he was, otherwise the story might have ended quite differently. As it was, it was almost tea time when Hedgie finally reached the door nestling in the tree roots. As far as he was concerned, it was the fastest journey he'd ever undertaken. In fact, he was quite exhausted when he staggered up the first few steps to the staircase.

In the dim interior, he missed a step and stumbled over something soft. Before he could work out who or what it was he had blundered into, he immediately caught his foot on another shape. He became so frightened, he rolled himself up into a ball and carried on through the staircase into space.

Turning over and over as he fell, Hedgie found to his surprise that he had landed on yet another soft object and he clung on instinctively. With a blood curdling shriek, the shape under him shot up into the air trying to shake him off, then took off down the pathway like a bucking bronco.

It must have been a nasty shock for the ginger cat. One moment he was comfortably dozing, hoping that a tasty young rabbit would present himself for supper from the maze of burrows among the tree roots, the next split second he was impaled on a cross between a bed of nails and a roll of barbed wire. The more he flung himself up in the air to free himself, the more Hedgie dug himself in the cat's fur.

At least, he'll take me somewhere, gasped Hedgie. But the speed they were going so frightened him, he shut his eyes and hoped it wouldn't be too far because he was beginning to feel a bit sick.

As they went on, the cat's prancing and leaping became so wild that Hedgie pressed even closer until his spikes became entangled in the cat's fur.

'Aaah!' screeched the ginger Tom, and shot ahead even faster, bouncing off trees and bushes in a mad effort to shake off his tormentor. But to no avail.

In a last desperate attempt, he threw himself into a pond. When he found he couldn't hold his breath any longer, he climbed wearily out on the other side, only to discover Hedgie was still there.

It was no good. With a final howl of frustration, the cat flung himself through the air, and went straight through the front door of a building looming up in front of them, leaving an outline of himself in the woodwork to show where he had been.

He landed, still howling, in the middle of a seething mass of brown rats, and a ripple of horror ran through the gathering to the very back of the barn.

Captain Mayfair, quicker than most to size up a potentially dangerous situation, took hold of Lola and slipped to the back of the make-shift stage where Black Freddie was addressing the troops, and ran up a flight of steps to the emergency exit.

Caught in the middle of his wind-up speech, Black Freddie signalled to his bodyguard to bring the prisoners, and hastily followed his example. His few trusted generals rushed forward to seal off the staircase to give him a chance to escape.

Meanwhile, time seemed to stand still as the ginger cat pulled himself up, still groggy, and gazed around astonished at the sight before him. Was he seeing things? A mass of snarling faces swam into his vision. He shook his head, thinking he was dreaming. All at once, the faces lazily clicked into focus, and his eyes nearly popped out of his head. He was so overjoyed, he forgot all about his prickly burden, and gathered himself to pounce. Sensing this, Hedgie nimbly let go and dropped to the floor out of the way. He knew when he wasn't wanted, and made his way to the nearest door.

Casting a final look behind, he chuckled at the pandemonium. Bodies were being flung everywhere. One even landed on his back – but they didn't stay long. A hedgehog's back is not everyone's idea of a soft landing, particularly when you have just had a knockout blow from a mad cat.

Only the ginger Tom was happy. He felt ten years younger as he gambolled around, leaving a trail of rats in his wake. It was getting so easy, he began swiping them with one paw behind his back to give them a sporting chance.

Chapter Nine

Out on a limb

Black Freddie cursed at the sounds of pursuit following him, signalling the end of his rosy dreams. At least, he would make sure of that meddling swine, Startup, if nobody else. The thought filled him with particular pleasure, more than compensating for the loss of his troops.

In front, Lola tugged at the rope viciously, making Startup wince. 'Not much farther for you,' she gloated, as the old oak tree came into view. 'This is where you'll swing - on that top branch for everyone to see.'

Startup struggled fiercely and as the procession slowed, Black Freddie hurried up. 'Who told you to stop – are you mad?'

Captain Mayfair pushed forward nervously, half checking for signs of pursuit behind.

'Lola's right, Freddie. We'll never get away with this lot holding us up. Why don't we get rid of them now?'

'Freddie?' growled Brown Rat menacingly. 'Who said you could call me that? I'm King Freddie to you. Keep moving, I've got something better in store for our young rabbit friends. Move!'

Muttering furiously to himself, Captain Mayfair obeyed. Although he had lost his troops, King Freddie was still a formidable force to be reckoned with, and being a natural coward at heart, the captain had no intention of arguing with him.

Inside the oak tree, Owl stirred. Overhearing the last remark, he re-doubled his efforts to free himself, before falling back exhausted. What seemed like an eternity passed, and then Owl came to and heard a slow measured approach of another animal. It could only be...

'Oh, do hurry up, Hedgie,' he sighed. 'This is no time to dawdle.'

Hedgie stopped and blinked. 'Is that you, Owl?'

'Well, if it isn't, I'm doing a remarkable imitation,' grunted Wise Owl. 'Stop chattering and cut me free. You can tell me what's happened afterwards.'

Without further ado, Hedgie did as he was told. He found a piece of Owl's mirror that the rats had broken, and started sawing at the ropes. While he was doing this, he told Owl what had happened, and Owl proceeded grimly to bring his friend up to date.

Hedgie fell back aghast. 'What can we do?'

Wise Owl struggled to his feet and rubbed his legs where the rope had cut into the flesh. 'I'll tell you what you can do. You can untie Oswald the Duck and get him to round up all the other animals in the barn and tell them to get to the bank as fast as they can. We still have time to cut them off. Meanwhile, I'll try and delay them, somehow.'

'But Owl,' protested Hedgie anxiously. 'You're in no condition to do anything. You should be resting.'

'Resting?' bawled Owl, with nearly all his old strength back. 'The day I rest, you might as well bury me, because I'll be no use to anyone. Now, you see to Oswald.'

'Oswald?' said Hedgie plaintively, peering into the gloom. 'I can't see anyone here, Owl.' He looked back, but in that short space of time Wise Owl had taken a few tottering steps and had bravely launched himself, disappearing in the dusk.

Shaking his head, Hedgie felt around with his spikes and hearing a muffled yelp decided it must be Oswald. 'Come on then, Oswald,' he said heavily. 'Let's hope it doesn't get dark too soon – otherwise it'll be sliced duck for supper.'

Afraid that the fleeing rats might be halfway back to their hideaway by now, Owl swooped awkwardly across the garden and made for the trees running down the side of the lane, hoping to intercept the enemy on the way.

'This is where they should be,' whispered Captain Mayfair, bending over and looking through the bushes. He peered across the lane at the river the other side.

'Out of the way, let me see,' snorted King Freddie, elbowing the others aside. 'Where's the fool gone now?' he demanded impatiently.

'I'm down here,' came a furious whisper from the Captain.

King Freddie leaned over. 'What are you doing down there, you cretin? I didn't say go down yet.'

'You pushed me,' was the strangled answer.

'Well, while you're down there, see if you can see the boat. If that idiot hasn't got here yet…'

Everyone's attention was focused on King Freddie, and for the first time there was nobody watching the prisoners.

It was all Startup needed. During the trek up from the barn, he had been wrestling with the knotted ropes behind his back and had somehow managed to get one paw free. Despite the pain, he hobbled across and grabbed hold of Prudence. On the way, he couldn't resist taking a passing swipe at King Freddie who overbalanced with a wild yell and disappeared from view. 'Aaaaah!'

Startup looked around for Puggles, and the smile was wiped off his face. His friend was boxed in by more brown rats bringing up the rear.

Before he could decide how to help, Puggles gallantly threw away any chance of escape by hurling himself at the rats and knocking them over with his vast weight. 'Get away,' he shouted, 'while I take care of this lot.'

Startup hesitated. Another minute and it would be too late. 'Hang on, Puggles,' he urged. 'We'll be back.'

While the guards watched the fight half mesmerized, the ground seemed to swallow the Rabbit up and Prudence too.

When at last King Freddie levered himself up over the top of the bank, he was livid. 'Where's the prisoners?' he spluttered. 'I'll have you lot fed to the fishes for this!' He glared at the terrified rats who shook their heads helplessly. 'You!' he thundered, pointing at Puggles. 'Where did they go?'

Only too happy to shift the blame, the cowering rats pushed Puggles forward.

Hiding his fear, Puggles winked mysteriously at the King Rat and motioned the others away.

King Freddie scowled, but took the hint and reluctantly led Puggles to the top of the bank out of earshot. He waited impatiently as Puggles straightened himself up. 'Well?'

Puggles whispered something inaudible and King Freddie bent forward irritably. 'What did you say, fat hog?'

Reacting, Puggles butted his tormentor in the waistcoat, sending him tumbling down the bank again. 'I may be a fat hog,' he shouted defiantly, 'but I am not a dirty rat!'

After a lot of scrabbling, an enraged ratty face peered over the top and glared speechlessly.

Before he could utter an order, a bored Lola glanced up from filing her nails, 'You should have let me deal with them. Then this wouldn't have happened.'

King Freddie went purple. Seeing him about to explode, Captain Mayfair stepped forward and said hurriedly, 'I think they went into that hole up the tree.'

'Eh, why didn't you say so before, you great twit?'

With a gloating laugh, King Freddie landed at the foot of the tree. 'If they're there, I'll find them, never fear,' he promised evilly.

Inside, Startup placed a finger on his lips and pointed upwards. Prudence nodded. Although they had managed to cast off the rest of their ropes, it was still awkward to use their muscles. So it was an agonising business trying to work their way up the inside of the trunk, with very few good holds to help them.

They had not gone very far when a triumphant yell from King Freddie told the others he had spotted them, and Captain Mayfair and Lola hurried inside to join him.

But before anyone else could follow, Puggles pointed dramatically up at the sky. 'Great spotted writings in the Heavens. Look at that!'

Accustomed to obeying an order without question, the brown rats did as they were told. After a few puzzled minutes, they looked down again to find him gone.

'Yoiks!' To their astonishment, he had only got as far as the tree. Without bothering to go any further, he was sitting down, more than generously covering the hole up.

Baffled by his behaviour, the rats made a concerted dive at him. With a broad grin, Puggles merely lifted a podgy leg, and sent the rats high in the air, scattering them in all directions.

'My round, I think,' panted Puggles. 'Right, who's next?'

After that, none of the rats appeared terribly keen to take up his challenge. They just sat there glowering at him and listening to the sound of pursuit up the tree.

Higher and higher the two rabbits climbed, their progress getting slower, until poor Prudence started slipping.

'I can't go on,' she faltered.

Startup took a quick look above his head. 'Not much more,' he pleaded. 'We're nearly up at the top.'

Glancing down to check the distance between them and their pursuers, he had a shock. King Freddie was much closer than he thought. And Captain Mayfair was not all that far behind.

He turned to Prudence. There was no question of them trying to reach the top now, he realised. Prudence was just about all in.

'Hang on,' he whispered. 'I'll help you.' As he pulled her up towards him, he suddenly felt a soft current of air on his back. He reached out into the shadows behind him and a piece of bark came away in his paw, revealing a small patch of light.

'In here, quick,' he directed. 'It's hollow...'

Without waiting for an answer, he pushed her through the hole in the branch and quickly followed, carefully replacing the lump of bark and holding it in place.

Startup listened to the rats scurrying past their hiding place, scarcely daring to breath. A few minutes later he heard King Freddie calling out impatiently, 'Has anyone come out at the top?'

'No,' a chorus floated up.

There was a hurried whispered consultation above, and Startup heard with sinking heart the order he's been dreading.

'Then search the tree from top to bottom - they're in there somewhere. I'll give a fortune to the rats that find them.'

With a whoop, the rats swarmed at Puggles from all directions at the news, looping a rope around him to stop him lashing out. Keeping well out of reach from his hefty back feet, they pulled him away from the hole and fought to get in first.

Startup froze as a heavy foot jarred against the piece of bark he was holding and the next minute he heard King

Freddie sit down on the ledge outside and call down to them.

'Hurry up, you miserable lot!' Then to Captain Mayfair and Lola. 'We might as well wait here and let them do some work for a change.' The others sighed with relief, and to Startup's horror one of them rested their whole weight against the bark, making it give.

With sweat pouring off him, Startup strained to keep it in place. Just as he was about to let go, he felt the position ease and someone – it sounded like Captain Mayfair – complained. 'It's not very comfortable here. Can't we move somewhere else? It feels as if I'm being pushed.'

'You'll be more than pushed in a minute,' threatened King Freddie. 'Another moan and I'll heave you over the side.'

After that it grew quiet, and Startup wiped his face. He was feeling distinctively jittery, and when a paw tapped him on the back he nearly jumped out of his skin. Prudence was beckoning and pointing along the branch in great excitement.

'This way,' she mouthed.

Startup nodded with rising hope. He cast a frantic look around and grabbed at another broken piece of bark, jamming it against the other one as a temporary hold.

The gloom gradually lifted as they scampered along, Prudence leading the way. Finally, she stopped and pointed. Above them, the pale evening light filtered through a broad crack in the branch.

Meanwhile, feeling bad tempered and uncomfortable, Lola prodded Captain Mayfair who jumped nervously and nearly knocked King Freddie off the ledge.

'Are we going to wait all night?' she snapped.

King Freddie bounded to his feet with a roar. 'If you don't keep her quiet, I'll send you back to Siberia!'

Lola drew herself up haughtily. 'Are you going to let that...rat talk to me like that?'

Captain Mayfair shrank back as King Freddie nearly burst out of his robes.

'Why, you impudent hussy!' he screamed. ' If I didn't have more important scum to catch, I'd teach you a lesson you wouldn't forget!'

Lola sniffed contemptuously. 'You, and whose army?'

Plop. Two of King Freddie's buttons burst off his waistcoat as he stumbled forward, filled with rage.

Captain Mayfair unfortunately chose that moment to rise up in a vain attempt to calm Lola, and accidentally knocked King Freddie against the blocked hole. The next minute he disappeared through the gap with a cry.

Startup heard the excited voices and groaned as he tried to squeeze through the gap higher up without success.

'Let me try,' begged Prudence by his side. 'I'm smaller.'

Rabbit gladly moved aside and got ready to push. If he could only get Prudence away, at least he could hold them off for a while.

'Now,' urged Prudence, and he gave an almighty heave.

She gave a joyful squeak and then she was up, scrabbling to get a firm grip on the branch outside.

Looking up, he noticed that in her efforts to get through, she had accidentally knocked a lump of bark away and the hole looked larger.

It was now, or never. Startup took one last look back at the advancing rats. There was a howl of rage as he made a desperate leap. For a moment, he hung there, halfway through the hole. Then he kicked out with a final wriggle, and his foot bounced off King Freddie's head, giving him the added lift off he needed.

He sat panting over the hole, waiting to get his breath back, but a vicious nip on his leg from below changed his mind and he hurried after Prudence.

A great shout went up from below as he came into view.

Prudence suddenly felt scared and wavered, and then the scenery opened up in front of her and she made an unexpected discovery. The branch they were on was so long that the end of it almost touched a tree on the far side of the stream. All they had to do was to jump from one branch to the other. Once they were down the other side, nobody could catch them.

'Look,' she called back gleefully, 'we can get down the tree over there.' She was so overjoyed, she waved impishly at the rats milling around at the foot of the tree, waiting to get at them.

The two rabbits sped on towards the end of the branch, slowing down only to jump over the small cluster of shoots on the way. All the time, the branch was getting smaller and smaller, but they didn't seem to notice in their haste to escape. By now, they were across the lane and halfway over the river. At that point, the slender branch began to sway, and without warning dipped under their weight. Prudence cried out, and started slithering away from him...

'Hold on,' gulped Startup, darting forward instinctively to pull her back. Then he froze as the branch gave way even further. He hastily retreated until with a great feeling of relief he saw it slowly come up again.

Startup put a brave face on it. 'You go first,' he encouraged. 'I'll wait here.'

'That sounds like a very good idea, Rabbit,' a silky voice purred. For there behind him was King Freddie, supremely confident that at last he had his most hated enemy within his grasp.

'Aren't you coming then?' called Prudence, her ears twitching anxiously at the sound of voices. The branch was so narrow she couldn't turn round, but she didn't want to go without him.

'I'm fine,' cried Startup hoarsely. 'You go - don't wait. The branch won't take both of us at the same time. I'll be right behind you.'

'... or below you,' sniggered King Freddie, idly slicing some small branches away with his sword.

Startup forgot about his tormentor. It suddenly became more important than anything that Prudence should get away, even if it meant...he couldn't.

'Hurry up,' he called out urgently. 'You're holding everything up.'

'All right' said Prudence reluctantly. 'But don't be too long.'

'I won't,' he promised, willing her on.

Prudence took a deep breath and tried again. This time the branch quivered but held steady, and the rabbit kept going.

To give her a better chance, Startup drew back, dangerously close to King Freddie, presenting him with a perfect target to practice on.

With bated breath, Startup watched his friends dart forward in a series of leaps and bounds to cover the last few feet to safety. A final spring left her poised in mid-air, as the branch sagged under her, then with an extra flick and twist of her tail she was across.

'Bravo,' sneered King Freddie, 'Till we meet again. I have big plans for that young lady,' he leered.

Startup turned on him grimly. 'You'll have to kill me first.'

'But, of course,' agreed King Freddie smoothly. 'Where would you like it to be?' He made an imaginary cross with his sword inches from Startup's face. 'The head or the heart?'

'You'll have to catch me first,' taunted Startup, carefully watching the tip of the sword, as he edged away.

Every time King Freddie rushed forward, Startup jumped back, just out of range.

'Keep still, Rabbit, blast you. How can I get you when you're prancing around like a squirrel?'

'Give up,' said Startup simply.

'I'll be damned if I will,' bellowed the enraged Black Rat, and launched himself in a frenzied attack that had Startup hopping back even faster. Suddenly he slipped and found the branch move under him, and a warning cry from Prudence told him he couldn't go any further.

The news was greeted with a cry of oily satisfaction by King Freddie, and he renewed his attack, throwing everything he had into it.

This is it, thought Startup, and hurriedly jumped up and down to avoid the sword as the blade sliced under his feet. But to his disappointment, his attacker cunningly stayed where he was. If only I could get him closer, thought Startup, it might put him off his balance...

'Is that the best you can do?' he asked cheekily. He slid back an inch and leaned forward invitingly. He could see King Freddie was hesitating about taking another step – and that was all he wanted. Unfortunately for Startup, one of the rats in the boat below had the inspired idea of switching on a searchlight just at that moment. It seared through the fading light, completely blinding the Rabbit.

A gloating smile played around King Freddie's mouth. He lifted his sword, and took up the classic position for the fatal thrust.

'No, Rabbit. *This* is the best I can do,' and he aimed at the Rabbit's heart. Just as the tip of the blade was about to make contact, there was a frightening squawk above their heads, accompanied by a flurry of wings, and a black shape swooped straight at King Freddie's head, completely putting him off his stroke. He brought up his sword blindly to fend off the attack, but the bird came in again and again from every angle.

The rats frantically moved the searchlight across, hoping to help King Freddie see his attacker, but it had the opposite effect.

'Turn it off, you dolts, I can't see!' he roared, and the searchlight beam wobbled and went out abruptly. The contrast was so shattering that he couldn't see at all, and waved his sword around helplessly.

Wise Owl, as indeed it was, took advantage of his confusion to alight on the enemy's paw and sink his beak in it.

'Ow!' shrieked King Freddie, and with an oath dropped his sword with a clatter. A single cry from the boat told them where it had landed.

Startup didn't waste another second. With a wild yell he jumped straight at his foe, and the two rolled over and over along the branch.

Captain Mayfair was too cunning to get involved in the fight, but as the couple fought and punched their way in his direction, he waited nervously for his chance.

Just then, one of them staggered up, and in the deepening gloom he saw it was Startup. Seizing his opportunity, he reached up and pulled hard at another branch over their head. It was just small and flexible enough to sweep down and hit Startup with a thump, making him see stars.

Rabbit reeled and clung onto the branch to steady himself. With a cry of triumph, Captain Mayfair ran up behind him to finish him off. Just as he was reaching out, Startup let go the branch which caught the rat full in the face and knocked him sideways.

Lola screamed and rushed forward, clawing and kicking. Then seeing the Captain fall, she jumped after him with a fearful cry.

'This is where you follow him,' leered King Freddie. Pulling out a knife hidden in his lining, he crawled towards Startup.

Poor Rabbit was still in a groggy state, and thought he saw four or five figures making their way towards him.
Which one shall I go for, he asked himself stupidly, then found he hadn't any energy left to do much about it anyway.

From above, Wise Owl summoned up all his remaining strength, and spreading his wings flew unsteadily into battle. Mistiming his approach, he managed nevertheless to crash sideways into King Freddie upsetting his aim, and then fell like a stone out of sight. It was all he could do, but it was enough.

A kind of black despair settled on Startup. His only friend was gone, and all because of him. For the first time in his life, the gentle side of Rabbit was swamped by an overpowering desire for revenge.

He tore into King Rat with everything he possessed, seeing only the face of Wise Owl sacrificing himself to keep him alive. Like Owl, Startup was no longer fighting for just himself but for all the village, and all he held dear.

Seeing his number was up, King Freddie tried all the dirty tricks he could think of, but his luck was fast running out.

'If I go - you go with me!' he screamed, grabbing at Rabbit as he slipped. Unfortunately for him, his grip fastened on something that came apart in his paws. For a brief second he bared his teeth in a hideous grimace, and then he was gone.

From the howling and wailing that floated up and the sounds of hasty departure, Startup knew as he clung there that the rat invasion was over.

It was not until later, when he made his way wearily down the tree that he realised what had saved his life. The lucky charm that Prudence had given him was no longer around his neck.

As he staggered out of the tree, he grinned at Puggles waiting for him. 'I hope it brings King Freddie better luck - wherever he is,' he croaked. Then he fainted.

Chapter Ten

Our postman

Now he was back in the fold of his family again, and being fussed over by all his old friends, Startup felt that nothing would ever be the same again. What he had been through in the past few days was enough to last any normal rabbit a life time.

Dora, his mother, did her best to understand, and so did his father after a fashion, but without much success.

It was all because of Grumps. Although Wise Owl was still alive, Startup was convinced it was all his fault. With the doctor fighting for Owl's life, he felt more guilty than ever.

'It's worse than losing him in the fight, somehow,' he confided wretchedly to Prudence. 'If only I had listened to him earlier — none of this would have happened.' It seemed as if he was under a suspended sentence.

'Nonsense,' said Prudence briskly, although she ached with sympathy. 'When he goes, it'll be the way he always wanted - fighting for what he believes in. The fact that he was helping his friends at the same time makes it a bonus as far as he is concerned. You must see that.'

'I keep telling myself that.' said Startup mournfully, 'but it doesn't seem to make any difference.' And he wandered off by himself to hide his sorrows.

Prudence fought against following him. 'It is something he will have to come to terms with,' she told Puggles sadly, then turned her head away quickly so that he would not see her tears.

'Don't worry,' said Puggles gruffly. 'Give him a chance to sort himself out.'

Old Pebble Eyes, the elderly stork consultant at the animal hospital, was not allowing Wise Owl any visitors, so Startup went off for a long walk by himself.

Wherever he went, the animals were sympathetic, for Grumps was well respected. But the talk was all about the new baby expected at Oak Tree Cottage, and Startup got fed up listening to it. Even his mother was full of it.

'Not long now,' she would say knowingly, and all her friends would immediately plunge into their own reminiscences.

So the weeks turned into months and then it was winter, and still the Wise Owl held on.

When the first flakes of snow appeared, it did not unduly worry Startup. He could see the pathway quite clearly, so he set off on his regular trip to the hospital to ask about Grumps. But the message was still the same as the day before. Unchanged.

It was 10 o'clock, and the pale morning sun had disappeared behind a cloudy yellow sky. And it was cold, bitterly cold.

Startup did not linger by the pond on the way back, where he used to see Clara Goose. As he carried on, he couldn't help thinking what a funny old stick Clara was.

Once news of Hare's betrayal had leaked out, Leonard decided it was time to go, and Clara had loyally stuck by him.

One hot summer's night she had collected all her savings – Hare had seen to that – and they eloped to a worker's commune, as Hare airily called it, near Islington, where his radical views were more fashionable.

The only thing Clara did object to, as she wrote to her Cousin Mabel, was that they expected her to share all her savings with everyone else. Naturally, I did no such thing, my dear, and I am extremely unpopular with them. Rather surprisingly, Hare agrees with me. However, you will be pleased to know that my husband has been asked to stand for local election. I have a feeling that one day he will be a great leader. Do tell the others, Mabel, because I would like them to feel he is well thought of, despite all those horrid things they said about him.

Startup halted and came out of his day dream. Everywhere he looked, the garden was covered with a thick blanket of snow, and all his footsteps had disappeared. As he stood there musing, a great white curtain blotted out Oak Tree Cottage only a dozen feet away.

As he struggled against the elements, tucking his head down to stop the snow getting into his eyes, he aimed at the direction where he had last seen the cottage. It was so deep in places that he had to leap high in the air to stop himself sinking out of sight.

Just as he was about to give up all hope of getting there, he ran slap into the back of the cottage, banging his nose on the brick wall.

Wait a minute, he thought, blinking through watery eyes. If I follow the wall round to the front, I should be able to get down the steps into the lane. Then it's only across the bridge and over the river and I'm home.

He nodded to reassure himself, and then started edging out round the corner where he was flung back by the full force of the snow storm. By now, he could hardly see the path, let alone the steps. It was all he could do to fight his way, inch by inch, to the front porch where he sank down exhausted on the doorstep.

While he was getting his breath back and wondering what to do next, he heard a swishing sound. The curtains above his head were pulled back, and a beam of light cut across the path. Above him a face peered out. It was George. He looked disgustedly at the snow coming down, and then drew back inside.

Before he closed the curtains again, Startup saw with interest that there was a large window box in front that acted as a wind brake and kept the snow off.

Risking instant discovery, Rabbit shook off the snow and jumped up into the broad shelter of the window ledge where he huddled against the window for warmth. Through a crack in the curtain he could see George pacing nervously up and down, casting a shadow on the window.

At the far end of the room, he could just see the young wife, sitting on the settee wrapped in a rug, smiling bravely at her husband every time he turned towards her.

The next time he wheeled around, her smile slipped and he stood there looking very worried. After some hard thinking, he squared his shoulders and came back past the window as if his mind was made up, and thundered up the stairs.

His wife winced at the bumps and crashes going on overhead, and after what seemed like hours, George came down again carrying a suitcase bursting at the seams, and set it down next to her.

'I'll bring mine down in a minute,' he told her.

'I'm glad you're coming with me,' she said in a matter-of-fact tone, but she looked at him lovingly as she said it.

George nodded and tried to smile reassuringly. Now the decision was made there was no hesitation, and he crossed to the telephone and dialled a number. There was a long pause, and then he dialled again, getting increasingly impatient. At last, he slammed the receiver down and went to the front door where he battled with the bolts. The gusting wind blew the door open with a bang, and great bursts of swirling snow engulfed him as he peered out

'The bally line must be down,' he called back tersely. Then half to himself he muttered, 'There's only one thing for it.'

'What are you doing out there, George?' his wife called.

Without replying, he slipped his wellington boots on as quietly as possible.

'George?' she said insistently.

'I'm just popping out for the doc,' he remarked casually.

'In this weather, it's crazy!' she protested, knowing there was nothing else he could do. 'Anyway, you can't go out without your overcoat – it's upstairs.'

George hesitated, then shrugged and went back inside. What followed was almost too quick for the eye to take in. He had only got halfway up the stairs when there was a slithering noise and a series of thuds and oaths. The next minute he came flying down through the doorway, arms flailing and hit the floor with a crash that rattled the window. Shortly afterwards a case followed him, and knocked him out, just as he was trying to get up.

Joan raised herself with an effort and tried to make it across the room, before giving up and sitting down again.

'Oh my darling, it was all my fault,' she cried. 'If I hadn't made you go upstairs...'

'I'm all right,' George shook his head gingerly, and gathered himself together to get up. As his face drew level with the window, he caught sight of Startup. His cry of astonishment turned into a quick gasp, and holding his leg he collapsed into a chair.

Fussing over him, Joan moved around in slow motion and tried to make him comfortable, but when she tried to straighten his legs he let out a yell that made Startup jump. She left him alone after that, and just picked up his case and slid it out of the way before anyone tripped over it.

'Well, I shan't be needing that,' he said heavily without thinking, and immediately regretted it. They both sat there silently for a moment letting the implications sink in.

Taking a deep breath, Joan got up slowly and quietly opened the window.

'Hallo, little one,' she said brightly. Then to George, 'Look, you've frightened the poor bunny.' Before he could object, she gently lifted the rabbit in and stroked his head.

'There you are, bunny,' she said shutting the window. 'I can see you don't like the snow either. I wonder what he's doing so far from home?' Her smile vanished, and she clutched her side.

'Oh, George, if the doctor doesn't come soon, we'll have to manage on our own.'

'Manage ourselves?' uttered George faintly. 'I can't even get up.' He stared broodingly at Startup. 'If only you were a pigeon, we could tie a message on you or something.'

'Wait a minute,' said Joan, an idea stirring. 'Hold on to him, will you?' She passed Rabbit over and made her way carefully to the mantelpiece, where she found what she had been seeking.

'This should do the trick.' It was a photograph of the two of them standing in front of the cottage the day they arrived. She quickly scribbled a message on the back and read it out.

'How does this sound? Urgent, please send the Doctor to Oak Tree Cottage at once. Joan Rich is having her baby, and George has injured his leg. Please hurry. Time: 6 pm.'

Her husband waved his hand helplessly. 'Great, but what good will that do? How are you going to get it to him?'

Joan gazed around pensively. 'Now, all I want is a piece of string - I know,' she undid a ribbon from her hair, 'This'll do.' Taking a pencil, she made a hole with it through the corner of the photograph, and then tied the ribbon to it.

'Yes, there we are – meet bunny, our postman.'

George raised his eyes to the ceiling, as if his wife had finally taken leave of her senses. Then realising she was serious, he tried to make a joke of it. 'Oh, yes of course. Come on Bunny, time for your walkies down to the village. And while you're there, just pop this note into the Doctor's letter box, will you? You'll recognise his door- it's got his name on the plate. That's jolly good of you old boy. Pull this off and you'll get some carrot tops, I shouldn't wonder.'

'Just hold him carefully, darling,' said Joan, ignoring his remarks. 'You may well laugh, but this little bunny...' she tied the ribbon around his neck, '...is going to be our special delivery.'

She opened the window and placed Startup on the ledge. 'Now, do your best. Daddy can laugh, but if you're a good boy I'll give you a great big bundle of carrots all to yourself. Off you go.'

For a moment, Startup sat there as she closed the window, and then moved uncertainly to the edge.

'And what good do you think that's going to do?" asked George, trying to move his leg without it hurting.

'Can you think of anything better?' said Joan simply.

George grunted. 'Why did we ever shut ourselves away in such a remote spot like this, in the first place?'

'Oh George,' she protested. 'You know we wouldn't have wanted to live anywhere else. I've been Rich in more ways than one, as the Vicar reminded us only the other day.'

George tried to smile. 'I know...it's just...if only that bally doctor would come, as he promised.'

'Darling,' she felt his forehead to see if he had a temperature. 'How could he have possibly come with all this snow about. Now he knows it's more urgent, I'm sure he'll think of something.'

Straightening him up in his chair, she said forgetfully. 'While we're at it, we'll need plenty of hot water, so go and put the kettle on, there's a dear...'

Her husband did not attempt to reply. He was too full for words.

In the freezing weather outside, Startup tried to make some sort of sense out of what he had seen. What am I supposed to do with this thing around my neck, he puzzled. If only his father had been there, they would have known what to do.

As he concentrated on the problem, he was disturbed by a funny sound coming from the top of the window box. First a little lump formed in the soil, then it got larger and out popped Spike, the worm. He took one look at the snow piling up and said, 'it's bad enough having to spend all my time digging underground, without finding stuff like this on top.'

Startup was envious. 'It's all right for you. You can at least get away from it all. Here am I with a message stuck around my neck, and I don't know what to do with it. Anyway, where can I go in this weather?'

Spike flicked a piece of root off his waistcoat. 'Oh, I expect they want you to go to the doctor. Everyone says the baby is due any time now.'

'Go for the Doctor?' repeating Startup blankly. 'In this weather - he's the other side of the village.'

'Well now,' said Worm thoughtfully. 'I can't go - the baby would have grown up before I get there. Tell you what though...' and he dived under the soil with a flick of his tail.

There was quite a thick layer of snow on the edge of the box, and when he reappeared Startup was getting colder than ever.

'All fixed,' he said cheerfully. 'Caw will soon be here - he'll help you.'

'Caw?' asked Startup crossly. 'Who's that?'

'Why Caw, the Crow, of course,' said Spike. 'He's a nice crow - do anything for you. You want to watch him though- he can't keep his claws off anything.'

Startup was impressed. He didn't like to ask Spike how he managed to get hold of a crow at such short notice. And indeed, how did he think the crow would be able to help him. He had heard the Hookwood worms were a clever lot, and besides he didn't want to look stupid.

True to his word, a big black crow wheeled into sight overhead and landed on the edge of the window box. He strutted up and down and seemed fascinated by the red ribbon around Startup's neck.

'Right, there you are,' said Spike, undeterred by the vast shape casting a shadow over them. 'Startup here wants to get to the Doctor in the village. D'you know the way?'

'Caw,' croaked the crow. His beady eyes fastened on the red ribbon again. 'I look after that, jah?'

Rabbit instinctively held on to the photograph, and then he had an inspired thought. 'No, but you can have the ribbon when we get there.'

The crow had to be content with that, but as they took off he kept casting a greedy eye on it.

'Goodbye, Spike,' called Startup. 'Thanks for everything.' Then they were swallowed up in a blinding snow storm that lifted them higher and higher, and battered at them continuously.

Clinging snowflakes hit Startup like a rain of bullets, filling up his eyes and mouth and ears until he couldn't see or hear anything. It was a terrifying experience.

They were now flying blind, and even the crow seemed to lose his sense of direction. After wheeling around uncertainly, he swooped low over some trees and discovered they were approaching the Church. Braking slightly, he corrected his flight path and cut across the field to the high street. As he peered down to see if Rabbit was still there, he caught a glimpse of the red ribbon again, blowing madly this way and that, until he became hypnotised by its brilliance.

'Aaah,' he croaked, 'You are mine.' And he bent down and picked at it feverishly.

'Hey,' gasped Startup, as the great beak snatched at his fur in his attempts to get at the ribbon. 'Stop it!' He swung his paw in a futile gesture, which left him hanging precariously by only one paw.

Caught off balance, the crow jerked its claw up to right itself, an action that weakened Startup's grip. He found his paw sliding off Crow's leg and he fell with a sickening swoosh, down, down. 'Now I know what Grumps felt like,' he thought inconsequently. As he turned over in the air, he saw the Church swimming lazily up towards him. 'At least I'll get buried in the right place,' he quipped. The next minute his mouth was full of snow again, and his body left an outline in the snow as he plunged into a deep snow drift.

'So this is what it's like in the great animal world above,' he thought. 'At least, it's comfortable here.'

Then as he found it more difficult to breathe, he changed his mind and started kicking out in all directions. 'Ouch,' he spluttered as his paw hit a hard object. 'That's not right - I shouldn't feel any pain, if I'm dead.' And he renewed his efforts, pulling himself up on the stone-like shape next to him. Just as he thought his breath was failing, he made a final despairing lunge and found himself free of the heavy weight on his chest. Immediately, he started coughing and heaving and...breathing. Breathing?

'I'm alive!' he shouted out and laughed. Actually, it sounded more like a croak, but he didn't care. He stayed there, inhaling pure fresh air, glad to be in the land of living again. Then he discovered he was sitting on a gravestone and patted it thankfully, getting his strength back. 'You saved my life, stone - whoever you belong to.'

After a while, he took more interest in his surroundings, and began to work out where he was. The Church was in front of him and he could just see the top of the lytch gate where the pathway came out overlooking the high street. If he could somehow get across that last gap, he could roll down the bank into the road, and then it was only a short distance to the animal hospital.

It was only then that he realised how hopeless his position was. The gravestone he was perched on was surrounded by snow and so were all the other headstones, as far as he could see. The pathway to the lytch gate probably ran past the very gravestone he was sitting on, but he couldn't use it. Once he jumped down and got trapped in the snow again he might as well give up. The memory of that ghastly sensation when he landed still haunted him.

A couple of sparrows alighted on a gravestone a few yards away, and seeing Startup they hopped a little distance away onto the next one. Their action gave him an idea. If they can do it, why can't I, he reasoned. He measured the distance again. I haven't got wings, he allowed ruefully, but my back legs should be strong enough.

With fast beating heart, he nerved himself for the ordeal. He tensed his leg muscles like coiled springs, and shutting his eyes launched himself wildly at the nearest headstone, peeping out of the snow like a stepping stone.

The shock of landing ran through his body like a battering ram, and he hung there undecided wondering what to do next. The longer he stayed, the more uncertain it became.

In the end, he made up his mind and set off boldly to take them all in his stride, following a zigzag course that carried him nearer and nearer to his goal. As he got halfway there, his tiredness overtook him and he grew a little careless, and misjudged his landing. His paws slid down the face of the headstone, and he nearly knocked himself out as he bounced off into the suffocating depths.

Terrified, he attempted to claw his way back, but couldn't find a support of any kind to help him. He floundered about, becoming weaker and weaker, until he really thought his last hour had come. Please spare me, he heard himself gasping. I only wanted to help those humans, and show Grumps I can be good sometimes.

In answer to his prayers, his foot touched on a soft springy hump and he clutched it, pulling himself up. His head broke the surface and a flood of relief swept over him, although he still couldn't see a thing. His delight quickly evaporated, for when he rubbed his eyes, he came face to face with a hungry looking fox sitting only a foot away on the last headstone in his way. He swayed there trembling, drained of energy, unable to believe his cruel luck. 'I don't suppose it would make any difference if I told you I was on my way to help someone,' he said wearily.

'Aren't we all,' replied the fox languidly. He reached out and lifted Rabbit towards him with effortless ease. 'What a credit we animals are,' observed the fox cordially.

'Here you are doing someone a good turn, and here am I doing the farmer a good turn as well. It's highly gratifying, isn't it?'

Startup nodded, frantically trying to think of a way out.

'Makes life worth living after all, doesn't it?' Fox continued. 'Ah well, all good things must come to an end sometime, I suppose.' He was just adjusting his grip on Rabbit, wondering which succulent piece to start on, when he spied the red ribbon dangling from his neck. 'Mm, Rabbit,' he enquired, loosening his hold to view it more closely. 'That really is rather intriguing. What exactly is it?'

Startup said the first thing that came into his head. 'It's a treasure.'

'Is it, indeed?' The fox's cunning eyes seemed to bore right through him. 'What sort of treasure?'

Rabbit's scattered wits started working again. 'I'll have to show you,' he said at last. 'It's all written in rabbit code on the card.'

'Hmm, well I'm waiting.'

'Not here,' said Rabbit quickly, not daring to lift his eyes and give the game away. 'Over by the lytch gate. There's no room here.'

The fox turned his request over in his sharp foxy mind, and examined it from every angle. 'You weren't thinking of escaping once we get there, were you, Rabbit?'

'Me?' Startup opened his eyes with all the innocence he could muster. 'How could I?'

'Right,' snapped the fox. 'Let us proceed. But I shall take charge of the treasure just in case...' He ripped off the photograph and scrutinised it.

'But fox, I can't get the lytch gate by myself,' cried Rabbit in a frightened voice. 'You'll have to carry me on your back.'

Fox fixed him with a searching look, but seemed satisfied.

So Startup clambered on his back, and the fox stretched himself for a lazy jump. Just as he was arching his back, Rabbit slipped the red ribbon off his neck and dropped it over fox's head. With a quick twist he tightened the ribbon, and the fox croaked and dropped the photograph right into his waiting paw.

Choking, the fox fell short and disappeared in the snow, and Startup ran up his back and jumped clear onto the lytch gate. He spared a brief backward glance to witness fox's legs kicking furiously in the air, and then he was running for dear life along the wall leading down into the high street.

He paused, overlooking the road. All was clear. With a sudden premonition he turned his head to see fox hurtling down the wall towards him. It was now or never. He said a quick prayer and dived onto the road, and ran as fast as he could straight for the hospital. He followed the deep tyre marks left by the traffic that kept him locked in the tracks. Soon he could hear and almost smell the fox gaining on him, forcing him to strain every muscle in his body to keep going.

Teeth snapped behind him, and with a supreme effort he flung himself clear. Then they came again and again, tearing fur out of his tail, then with a terrible crunch sinking into his back leg. Startup rolled over and over, fighting to get away while the fox harried and bit him, now almost playing with him, waiting to finish him off.

The interruption, when it came, was sudden and something neither of them expected. A horn blared, brakes squealed, and there were shouts in the distance. Then a spray of snow hit them, and Startup was tossed high in the air. When he landed on the ground again, all the breath was knocked out of him, and he lay there unable to move. He heard a voice saying, 'Stupid animal ran right out in front of me. I didn't have a chance.'

'Poor devil, he's a goner, I reckon...'

'Make way there - give the ambulance some room...'

Then a blinding light picked him out, and he heard whispers all around him, buzzing in his ears. The ground no longer felt hard. He was so light, he was floating...

When he came around again, the buzzing was louder and opening his eyes he saw Old Pebble Eyes peering down at him short - sightedly.

A bubble of laughter filled Rabbit's brain. 'I couldn't be in better hands,' he thought drowsily. 'All he needs are some glasses,' and he drifted off to sleep.

The next time he woke, his father Ben was sitting there, clutching his pipe anxiously.

'The message...' murmured Startup thickly, feeling for the ribbon.

'Don't worry, son, it's all been taken care of. I was there when they brought you in. We found the note all right.' He swallowed. 'Fair put the wind up us, you did.' Then to lighten things he tried to chuckle and nearly choked. 'They got that village Doctor, old Bumble, up there in one of them flying machines. He's more scared than the patients, I shouldn't wonder. Can't stand flying, you know.'

Startup tried to raise his head. 'And...Grumps. How's Grumps?'

'Ask him yourself,' said Ben, his eyes twinkling. With that, he moved his chair to one side so that Startup could see across to the next bed.

In his lazy state, all he could make out was a blur of a face that kept sliding out of focus.

'So they thought they got you too, eh Rabbit?' the voice was weak but unmistakable.

'Grumps!' managed Startup faintly. 'You're all right then.' He felt a funny warble in his throat as if it had got clogged up, and the tears were coursing down his face.

Old Ben furtively wiped a tear away and fumbled with his pipe.

Owl barked with a touch of his old humour. 'Take more than a bunch of rats to kill me off, boy. I'm good for a hundred yet - if old Pebble Eyes doesn't get me first.'

Startup sank back with a sigh of relief. Everything was hoppity good again.

His father spluttered happily over his pipe, then suddenly remembered where he was and stuffed it away in his pocket.

'Bless me, the boy's gone to sleep again.' He winked at Wise Owl. 'Looks like I can go and have my lunch after all.'

After that, well there's not much left to tell. Just as all the Hookwood animals were sitting down to a hot lunch, a buzzing noise could be heard in the sky and a little speck in the distance grew larger and larger. The next minute, a helicopter swooped down at treetop height, its rotor blades clacking, scattering birds left and right.

There was great excitement as it hovered over Oak Tree Cottage, and greater excitement still as two figures were lowered out of the doorway onto the small square of lawn beneath. After they landed, two bundles with poles sticking out were sent down after them and were taken into the cottage.

Most of Hookwood were gathered in the trees to watch open mouthed as Joan and George were brought out and carefully winched away. Then the two men seemed to be arguing about something and a third stretcher was signalled. A ragged cheer went up when the two finally left the ground, and the animals thought it was the best treat they'd had since the Fair.

When the last of the crew clambered on board, the navigator asked, 'Who was the other stretcher for, Jack?'

'For the Doctor, of course,' was the laconic reply. 'It was the only way I could get him up again.'

At that point, they had to get the Doctor out of the stretcher rather quickly, because not long after that the healthy cries of a baby could be heard. And there are some animals in Hookwood who will tell you to this day without blinking that they heard the baby over the noise of the helicopter's engines.

Joan was bursting with pride when Bumble lurched across the rather cramped space, and handed over the tiny bundle for her to hold.

'I never thought we'd have our first child in a helicopter,' she smiled at her husband.

George attempted a smile, and clutched at his tummy. 'And the last, I hope.'

'And I never thought I'd have to travel in a helicopter to deliver one, my dear,' said Bumble nervously, collapsing into the nearest canvas seat.

'Oh, I believe this is for you,' he remembered, passing over a crumpled photograph.

'D'you see that, George?' thrilled Joan, waving it at him. 'He did get through, after all.' She turned to the baby and whispered, 'One day, my little one, we'll tell you all about that brave little rabbit who's going to get the biggest bunch of carrots he's ever seen in his life.'

-ENDS-